THE UNIDENTIFIED

RAE MARIZ

BALZER + BRAY

An Imprint of HarperCollins*Publishers*

Balzer + Bray is an imprint of HarperCollins Publishers.

Library of Congress Cataloging-in-Publication Data
Mariz, Rae.
    The Unidentified / Rae Mariz.—1st ed.
        p.   cm.
    Summary: In a futuristic alternative school set in a shopping mall
where video game–playing students are observed and used by corporate
sponsors for market research, Katey "Kid" Dade struggles to figure out
where she fits in, and whether she even wants to.
    ISBN 978-0-06-180209-6
    [1. Identity—Fiction.   2. Corporate sponsorship—Fiction.   3. Alterna-
tive schools—Fiction.   4. Schools—Fiction.   5. Science fiction.]
I. Title.
PZ7.M33913Un   2010   2009054254
[Fic]—dc22   CIP
                                                                   AC

Typography by Sarah Hoy
12 13 14 15 16   CG/RRDH   10 9 8 7 6 5 4 3 2 1
❖
First paperback edition, 2012

For AK

X PRESS <START>

If reality TV cameras were installed in my high school, they would be focused directly on the Pit. That's where all the drama plays out.

Or wait, they've probably got cameras there already. All the security cameras from when the building was a mall, before it got converted into a school, before it became a site for the Game. Everyone knows we are being watched. It's not even something to be paranoid about. It's a fact.

What I mean is, everybody acts like they're on TV. Like we're stars in our own private dramas. We'll be talking to a friend and then all of a sudden, we're AWARE of . . . I don't know, being public. We start to say our lines too loud, waiting for the audience to laugh. Not for our friend to laugh,

1

just . . . the world. The world is watching, somehow. And we want to entertain them. We want to be smart and funny. Clever, witty, loved.

We want to know someone cares.

We know the sponsors care. They invest in the schools because they care about what we wear, what we listen to, what we watch—and what we're saying about what we wear, listen to, and watch. The cameras aren't there for surveillance, they're there for market research.

The world is a giant squinty eye, peeking in through the skylight, spying.

Does that creep us out? No. We like the attention.

1 CHOICES

We couldn't agree on what to play. Mikey, me, and Ari. As always, the hi-def screens lining the Pit were flashing advertisements for classes, hyping workshops on the different floors, trying to get kids to log on to the sponsors' featured activities for the day.

Mikey stared over my head, his attention glued to the nearest screen. They were showing highlights from the Robot Combat Arena up in the DIY Depot on the fourth floor. Cinematic sparks flickered on the screen as scrap-metal robots engineered by kids here in school slammed into one another. Bam bam bam. Each machine trying to flip, stall, or destroy the others.

The tinny sound of gears shrieking and crunching-metal

groans escaped from the speakers. The noise mixed with the already impressive decibels of laughter and chatter rumbling in the Pit.

Someone tried to squeeze past my chair and her loaded backpack whacked me in the back of the head.

"Hey, watch it," I said, turning to glare at the violator of my personal space.

The tiny girl looked up from her intouch®. She mumbled a kind of apology that got lost in the noise, and ran to catch up with someone.

She was obviously one of the newbies just getting started playing Level 13–17 in the Game. First off, she wore a *backpack*. That, like, shouts, *I'm new and have no clue*. Another few months and she'll be trading it in for a designer handbag, just to survive.

"Oh my god. That was Palmer Phillips's little sister," Ari said, craning to get a look at her. "You'd think that since her brother's the spokesman of Generation Triple-A she'd have a little more . . . I don't know, sense? Look at her."

The little sister of the most popular guy in school was wearing a pink hoodie polka-dotted with cartoon ponies and brown pants cut off at the knees. Her hair was pulled back into a classic prepubescent hairstyle, the messy ponytail. I'd never have guessed she was related to Palmer, "a metrosexual masterpiece," as Ari liked to say. Except maybe the eyes; they had the same almost-amber eyes.

"What's her name?" I asked Ari.

"Who?" she said, clicking through something on her notebook®.

"Palmer Phillips's little sister."

"Oh, Lexie. I think." She glanced back at the girl. "It's so weird to think we were ever that clueless."

"Yeah," I said, agreeing with Ari, even though I didn't.

I thought it took a lot of guts for her to ignore the Level 13–17 catalogue so completely, especially since her brother practically published the thing himself. The online catalogue featured all the latest of the latest trends in the Game; what the top players were wearing, listening to, linking to, watching. What they were *doing*.

Lexie was talking to a bore-core girl slouched in a chair a few tables away who didn't seem to follow the prevailing fashion advice either.

She was about my age—probably playing Level 15 and old enough to know better. Her shaved eyebrows were painted like exclamation points above her not-amused eyes. It was definitely a look designed to make you look . . . away. I wouldn't say she was fat, but Ari might less-than-tactfully mention that she was on the wrong side of her ideal body weight.

I couldn't imagine what someone like Lexie Phillips had to say to someone like her.

"Hey! Look at this!" Ari said, turning her notebook® so I could read the screen.

My eyes flitted over the text. It was an article on confidence-building makeup tips. The girl in the photo looked like she was going to leap off the screen and eat me. Chomp, chomp. Was that how you're supposed to appear assertive? She just kind of looked hungry to me.

Ari had already spilled the contents of her bag out onto the white tabletop, looking for something, trying to get me interested in a grab new cosmetics brand.

"This kohl-colored eyeliner would look amazing with your skin tone," she said, holding up a stubby pencil.

I was doubtful.

"Come on, Kid. This will give your face some definition. You know, make you look *significant*."

She squinted at my face, pushed my hair back, touched my cheek. I tried to enjoy the affectionate gestures and ignore the critical look she was giving me. Her eyes scanned over my forehead and eyebrows, the areas around my eyes, but never looked into them. It made me feel way insecure.

I hoped Mikey would come to my rescue, but he was still watching the screens, staring at the violent machines.

I sighed and gave in to Ari's makeover madness. I would do anything for Ari. She dragged the liner across my lower lash line. My eyes started to water.

Ari set the built-in camera of her notebook® to the mirror function and turned it toward me when she was finished. A girl I barely recognized blinked back at me from the screen. The eyeliner kind of made it look like I got punched in the face two days ago. If that was supposed to make me feel confident, it, um . . . wasn't working.

Mikey glanced away from the monitor during the

commercial break and caught my eye. Not that he could've missed it. I felt uncomfortably conspicuous.

"Nice," Mikey said, and reached over to grab Ari's eyeliner. "Do me! I want to look like a sad zombie clown too."

"No way. I'm not wasting any product on you."

Mikey tried different tactical maneuvers to wrestle the pencil out of her hand, but Ari was tenacious like a pit bull puppy. He couldn't break her grip.

I covertly smudged the stuff off my eyes and noticed that the bore-core chick with the eyebrows was sitting alone at her table again, watching the crowd in the Pit with calculated disinterest. Her gaze wandered over Ari and Mikey's wrestling match, stopping for a moment on me before she slumped back in her seat and made a big display of how to develop "the yawn" into a lifestyle accessory.

Ari finally let Mikey have the pencil and saw me watching the antiscenester girl.

"Someone should tell her apathy went out of style with shotgun suicides," Ari said. Then she stood up. "You want me to tell her?"

I grabbed her arm. "No, wait." I glanced at the girl in gray again. "Maybe boredom is retro?"

Both Ari and Mikey laughed at me.

"Listen," Ari said. "Jaye told me the whole sulky subculture thing is so over. So over. It's easy to be a mopey loser, but playing to win takes style. Want to see my victory dance?"

She made a motion like flicking open a cigarette lighter.

Extending first one thumb, then the other, until she was sitting there grinning with a two-thumbs-up gesture. She called this move "uncorking the champagne."

I groaned. "Don't. Ari, please."

Ari started humming triumphantly out of tune and did a jerky dance in her seat, waving her thumbs around. She did an unconvincing robot dance, then tossed in some weird, wiggly, snake-charmer kind of moves.

"Yeah, I don't need to see this," Mikey said, getting to his feet. "I'll be in the Park. Call me when the show's over, Kid."

"OK. Don't forget to sign us up for Studio time."

Mikey nodded and walked away. He didn't have much patience lately for Ari's near-constant need for attention and ego-stroking.

I waved to his back as he left us.

Ari continued with her dork-bot dance moves, unfazed. I tried to ignore her, but it was impossible.

"OK. You win!" I laughed and did a few dorky dance moves to make her happy.

Ari was what all the Craftsters called *manga*. You know, comic cute, all animated and exaggerated. Ari pinky-swears to the world that she spent the first two years in the Game sporting geek-chic fashion, but for that to be true you'd have to drop the "chic." Ari had been a no-win nerd, and in moments like these I could still see that the geek queen reigned supreme.

Ari knocked down her bubble tea with an overly enthusiastic elbow.

"Ah, dammit," she muttered, tipping her cup right side up. All the tiny tapioca balls settled back to the bottom. Little pools of orange neon speckled the table where the milky tea had splooged out of the straw. A puddle of the stuff inched menacingly toward Ari's notebook®.

"My stuff! It's getting all sticky!" she said, nearly hyperventilating.

"Hey, don't freak out," I said, rescuing her notebook® from the goo.

I grabbed a bunch of napkins and helped her wipe off her intouch®, makeup collection, and a bunch of retro Hello Kitty shit before putting it all back in her bag.

"What are these?" I shook a prescription pill bottle, newly de-gunkified.

"Vitamins," she said sarcastically, throwing them back in her bag.

She tossed the wadded-up napkin toward the trash can. It followed a tragically parabolic path to the floor, coming to rest nowhere near its target.

"Nice shot. All the sporty footwear cool hunters are totally going to be swarming you with skills like that."

Ari laughed, a little too loudly. "Shut up," she said and quick-sipped her bubble tea. She swallowed, then slapped the table with her hand, looking at me, eyes wide. "Hey! Did I tell you I started kickboxing?" She leaned back in her chair again. "I started kickboxing. It's so effing zen."

I stared at her stumpy fingernails while she played with that fat straw. She just got her nails done. They were painted with photo-repros of this season's top ten *Idol* contestants. As they got voted off the show, they got painted over on Ari's nails. Lucky for me, because I didn't follow the show, I could just glance at Ari's fingertips and know what everyone was talking about.

"Kid? Did you hear me?" Ari said, kind of annoyed that I wasn't hanging on her every word. "I *said*, you'd be surprised how much pep you get knowing you can break someone's knees, just like—" She started kicking my legs under the table.

We're best friends and I have the bruises to prove it.

I pulled my legs up onto the chair, where Ari couldn't reach them, but she had already lost interest. She was watching a group of girls make their way across the Pit. The crowd shifted slightly to welcome them into their midst. Everyone knew who these girls were. They were Fashion Fascists. These girls were the sponsors' darlings. They were all on the It List, every one of them branded.

The Fashion Fascists made their way through the crowd, announcing clique critiques in whispers meant to be heard. Eva Bloom, the dainty dictator herself, walked with them, not saying a word. Her disinterest in other people was generally more devastating than her insults.

"Palmer Phillips is just all credit. So hot," Quelly Atkins said above the clicking of the herd's high heels. The others cashed in their agreement.

"I can't believe he's going out with that Craftster skank Roksana Wronski."

"Only because she won that FreshFlash® photo contest. After the promo thing she did, they *had* to brand her," Quelly said, examining the ends of her cinnamon red hair.

"You mean that *porno* thing," Ashleah Carter snarked.

Their cutting laughter seemed to carry over to our table on a powdery cloud of girl-smell, a mix of fruity and vanilla-perfumed magazines.

I watched Ari to see how she'd react to the Fascists speaking smut about her friend Rocket. She behaved pretty much as expected, picking up her intouch® and fanning the clique flame wars.

aria: echo just called you a skank @ROCKET

"Anyone notice how anti-fat she's getting?" Quelly said almost wistfully. "I swear I could see vertebrae."

"Whatever. Fame is a fickle . . . um . . . something," Echo Petersson said, looking at the designer shoes her sponsors had hooked her up with. "She just better watch her back."

"Palmer needs to drop her. Hard."

"Yeah, on her face. Like Cayenne," Quelly said, laughing.

"Who?" Eva said coldly, her one syllable completely voiding the poor girl's existence.

The giggling group of Fashion Fascists marched past. Ari watched them go.

"Choke. Gag. Retch," she said in a sardonic staccato. "Those little Hitlers are going to stink up the Sweatshop with that poison." She pinched her nose and continued in a nasally whine, "They should get charged, like, emissions credits or something." She read her intouch® and laughed. "Rocket's so pissed about what they just said. She's up on the fourth floor and about to pollute their moisturizer supplies. . . . Hey, are you listening to me?"

I wasn't listening to her. I was watching a bird land on the planter by the trash can. It dive-bombed this other bird, then fluttered back up into the "trees" in the Pit. I tried to tap out the rhythm of its wing beats on the table-top. It gave me an idea for a new song.

It's weird that the starlings were in the Game at all. They were an uncontrollable element in an otherwise carefully designed environment. The blackbird scavengers grew fat and sassy on the food remains of hundreds of sloppy teenagers and there was nothing the administrators could do about it. Those cute and ruthless little bastards perched on tables and stared, defiant and unblinking.

I watched the birds fly up to the skylight, but lost them in the glare. The sky outside was white. Blank-screen boring.

Up on the fifth floor, I saw two or three people fooling around by the railings. The figures moved like silhouettes against the featureless white sky, like shadow puppets dancing. Or wrestling. Or—

The hairs on my arm electric-tingled. One of the puppets, one of the people, fell.

I held my breath, all the noise in the Pit stopped. This was not happening.

Someone had pushed a body over the edge. And it was falling.

Ari didn't see it, her attention was back on her notebook® mirror. She was making faces at the screen, fixing her lip gloss and stuff.

The body landed with a dull thud maybe ten feet away from us.

Thick red goop splattered when the body hit the ground, graphic horror film–style. A girl screamed and people stood up on chairs to get a better look.

Where the head should've been, there was just a red splatter mark, like a burst water balloon. A sign taped to the back of the dummy's sweater read:

UNIDENTIFIED. CHOOSE YOUR SUICIDE.

I turned away, but Ari didn't react. She just stared at the figure lying facedown on the ground.

A piece of the burst balloon face rested by my sneaker toe. The face was drawn on with black ink Sharpie. Shriveled up on the floor, it looked desperate and defeated. I picked it up.

Ari checked her clothes for stains. Drops of splatter glistened on her chin. "What do you think they're selling?" she asked.

2 ADVICERTIZE

Rumors and buzz rippled through the crowd as if the body had been a pebble thrown into a pool of water.

Kids were inching their way up to the dummy body, taking low-res pictures of the aftermath, then leaving.

Until the disturbance faded away into nothing.

Ari was sure that it was a school-sponsored publicity stunt. She was only interested in it long enough to register that it was a bad publicity stunt, because she didn't know what she was supposed to buy.

"Fail," she said in a jaded voice, looking around to see if anyone was interested in her opinion.

But I wasn't sure. There was something raw and clumsy

about the spectacle that corporations just didn't know how to imitate.

I guess I wanted to know what they were selling as much as everyone else . . . but I also wanted to know who *they* were.

Ari was hunched over her intouch®. Her rapid thumb movements pounded out a text message, probably to one of the Craftsters. She snorted back laughter, then pressed Send.

My intouch® buzzed when she uploaded since I was subscribed to her stream. She had written:

aria: i think i know who took your dress form @ROCKET

"You think *that's* Rocket's dress form?" I asked, taking a closer look at the lifeless body.

Ari looked up. "What? No." She glanced again at the dummy corpse. "No way. That's not even close to her measurements. All the Craftsters made mannequins with our individual body shapes, and someone took Rocket's last week from her work station. I bet Quelly took it."

Ari went on to explain some ongoing Sweatshop drama. I was disappointed that she thought a misplaced mannequin was a more interesting whodunit than a body dropped from the fifth floor.

"Besides," Ari said, "you shouldn't comment on people's private conversations, Kid. It's rude."

"Right. Sorry," I mumbled.

"And it just leads to misunderstandings, which can cause emotional trauma, and result in mental anguish . . ." Her voice trailed off as she checked her intouch®. I didn't know what Rocket replied since I wasn't on her stream, but Ari said, "Hey, I need to go up to four. You coming?"

"No," I said, still looking at the dummy corpse. "No, I have a meeting with Winterson. But you're coming to the Studio later, right?"

Ari did that thing she does when she's kind of annoyed. She shakes the hair out her eyes really fast, sighs dramatically, and does a kind of half-shrug, sending her bracelets hula-hooping into irritated little orbits around her wrists.

"I guess."

I took one last look at the body. At the shape of the splatter mark, kind of bird-wing shaped. Then I started walking to the other side of the first floor, to Carol Winterson's office.

I felt ridiculously sorry for it, the dummy. That no one cared that it ended its life for some unknowable reason, and now it was just lying there waiting for the cleanup crew to mop up its goo. Then I had to remind myself that it was fake. Not real.

Carol Winterson was my advisor. She was forty-mumble years old, but kind of new to the Game. I heard she had worked as a teacher in one of the last unaffiliated schools, but took the position because she wanted to be where the students needed her most. Which didn't make any sense. The Game gave us everything we wanted. It was *designed* to do that.

The Game started when the government admitted they had zero funding for education and the sponsors swooped in to invest in "the future." They set up Game locations all over the nation, like chain stores, to guarantee that the quality of education would be consistent at all sites. This new system was good for the government, good for the economy, good for the students. A win-win-win situation, as they said in the marketing literature.

"Katey. Come in, have a seat. I'll be with you in a sec."

Winterson had the phone cradled between her shoulder and ear while she was trying to type something. The sponsors didn't bother hooking up the counselors and educators with their latest tech swag. They saved all the best toys for the kids.

I rubbed my thumb against my intouch®, felt it purring in my pocket with news. I ached to pick it up and check the updates, but Winterson asked students to keep them off in her office.

I watched her fumble around with her ghetto technology, gray strands streaking through her frizzy dark hair like rocket trails in the night sky. She was clueless, but it could've been worse. I could've been stuck with someone semisavvy. One of those advisors who weren't much more than failed cool hunters, roaming around the school with their hip hairstyles that were grab like maybe six months ago. Someone like Ari's advisor, Jaye, who was more interested in hearing about self-esteem issues and asking leading questions on how we felt about the sponsors and school policies than providing educational guidance.

I tried to listen in on Winterson's phone conversation. Whoever she was talking to, it sounded like they were talking about me. Or I could just be a paranoid egomaniac, I don't know. But the talk was overly cryptic, a lot of *mmhmms* and glancing my way. The shadows in the corners of her mouth meant Winterson was pissed and bad at hiding it. She hung up, painfully civilized.

"Sorry about that, Katey. Let's see now." She squinted at her screen. "How's things?"

"Fine, I guess."

I dug around in the bowl of corporate candies Winterson kept on her desk, trying to find something not gross. She turned slightly and peered over her shoulder at the surveillance camera behind her before focusing on the screen again.

"Your scores are looking good," she said. "You're riding high on the bell curve."

"Yay. I'm average," I said, waving a cherry-flavored lollipop in sarcastic celebration.

Winterson's lips tightened into a sympathetic smile.

I looked down and wrestled with the candy wrapper. No matter how much time I dedicated to playing the Game, it didn't feel like I was the kind of person who was ever going to get high scores.

"I see you got bonus points for speed on six of your last

ten PLAY missions," she said. I know she was trying to be encouraging, but it made me feel like a bigger loser.

"Yeah, I've been trying to solve the clues fast to get the time bonus. To save up score credit for completion prizes or whatever."

"Is there a particular prize you have your eye on?"

The sponsors donated products to an end-of-year auction where the players with the highest scores could cash in their points for prizes after they completed their seventeenth and final level of the Game. I was still only on Level 15, but all the scores add up, so if I kept performing at this degree of dazzling mediocrity I would probably be able to afford like a "thanks for playing" button or something.

"My mom is hoping I can get enough points for the free ride scholarship." It was a bundled package with prizes from restaurant and real-estate sponsors for everything I'd need for living a whole year in the city after I left the Game. "But I'd really like recording and mixing gear for a home studio. Not that I'll ever have the score for any of that, but . . ."

Winterson nodded and made a note in her computer.

"I see you've made some changes to your profile."

"Yeah, you noticed?"

"It's been flagged as 'insufficient use of Network page' by the administrators."

I almost choked on the fruity juices of the lollipop. "What? I'm not blowing off my content assignments. I uploaded some songs Mikey and I wrote a few weeks ago, and I just did that essay-review for media literacy score."

"I know. Your Game content is fine, but they're *concerned* about the status of your Network page. Here, under the About Me section, you wrote 'None of the above.'"

I felt strangely embarrassed. I mean, I knew administrators monitored our pages—it was where we uploaded all our content assignments to be evaluated for score—but I didn't think they would make a big deal about what I wrote in the About Me section. I knew other kids who'd written much worse.

"So?" I would've left it blank if I could. I couldn't think of anything clever to put there, didn't really know how to describe myself to potential viewers of my profile. "Aren't we allowed to edit our pages?"

"It was such a dramatic change though," she noted. "It alerted the administrators that there might be an issue you wished to discuss with me. A lot of identifying content had been removed. Have you recently had a falling-out with a friend?"

Our Network profile pages were created when our parents registered us for the Game. They supplied all the facts and details during sign-up, but we were supposed to be free to mod our layouts to express our aesthetics. I had never really been into code accessories so I'd always let Ari design my page.

She made the background photo collages of the two of us together, and maybe a lyric we'd written or something. It was sweet. But lately I noticed she had been putting things on my page that seemed more like she was describing the person she wished I was instead of who I was. So I tried to do it myself, and apparently failed at that, too.

Winterson struggled to swivel her screen toward me to show me my Network page. I barely glanced at it; I knew what it looked like.

Compared to the tricked-out layouts and designs of other kids' pages, it was pretty pathetic.

"Your stated interests are: 'friends, music, and mysteries,'" she read from the screen.

"Yeah, so? That's all true."

"I know, Katey, but don't you think you could be a little more specific? Even your friend list is much less defined than a girl of your social capabilities should be. Why don't you share more of your interests and activities? People want to get to know you."

I made some noncommittal noises. I didn't really know why, but it felt too complicated to make public things that were important to me. Or maybe I was just frustrated because it felt like I couldn't express what was important to me even when I really tried.

"The administrators are worried about your failure to engage."

Failure. It was official. I was a loser. It practically said so in my record. I played with the scrap of latex I'd picked up at the crime scene so I wouldn't have to look at Winterson's concerned expression. The face drawn on the balloon piece looked the way I felt. Like this:

•_•

21

"Why do they care?" I said, stretching the rubber until it snapped back on my fingers. "Ow."

Winterson cleared her throat, then said, "The administrators need to have more insight into your interests to better tailor the Game to your needs."

She said the words as if she were reading them from a teleprompter, overarticulating each syllable.

"Are you upselling?"

Winterson's laugh sounded almost bitter. "This is your education, not fries and a Poke® cola."

I just sat there staring at the inscrutable balloon face.

"Katey?" Winterson said.

"Yeah?" I looked at her. The speckled iris of her eye. The wrinkle at the corner of her mouth. The stripes of her shirt. Her chewed pinky nail.

"Is something wrong?"

"What? No, it's just . . ." It wasn't my fault that I couldn't articulate my feelings with a cleverly designed app, or that when I added up points on personality quizzes I didn't recognize the person they described me to be. It's not like I *liked* being this average, this unremarkable. I blurted out, "You don't think the sponsors would ever try to sell suicide or something, do you?"

"What?" she looked genuinely surprised, and maybe a little scared. "You're not, um, in the market for a product like that, are you?"

Oh Google, she thought I was suicidal. "No, no no," I assured her and told her about the dummy suicide in the Pit.

She watched me carefully, then said she hadn't heard anything about it. "I don't agree with the sponsors on a lot of things, but I doubt they would ever advocate the sale of suicide to kids."

Her assurances were disturbingly unconvincing, though. I think it was because Winterson herself was disturbingly unconvinced.

3 TRICKSTER

I left the meeting with Winterson kind of weirded out. I couldn't decide what was worse, that the dummy drop was something the sponsors might have organized, or that it was some completely random person's idea of a good time.

I glanced at the wide, gray double doors that led to the headquarters, where the school administrators had their offices. The people working back there never came out into the Game, and kids never went in there unless they were sick or in trouble. Mikey had been in a few times for some stupid stuff. He just got too rowdy sometimes.

I stopped by the Pit again. Everything looked so different. I half expected to see a chalk outline, or yellow DO NOT

CROSS tape. OK, I knew they didn't call the cops for dummy suicides. Protecht security, maybe.

But still.

The goop was gone, no signs of the PR prank. I looked up at the railings on the fifth floor, where I had seen the struggle—at least two people messing around by the railing. Even that looked different. The sun had come out, and the blue sky made everything seem impossible.

I'd been thinking of the whole thing as a suicide because of the note on the back: UNIDENTIFIED. CHOOSE YOUR SUICIDE. But it wasn't a fake suicide. Someone up there pushed the body over. It was more like a mock homicide.

Sick.

I checked my intouch® for updates I missed and to see if anyone was commenting on the PR prank.

#spons: swiftx has high score on buy sell & destroy. beat him in the arcade.

mikes: is going to smash this 360flip. doubters, get fuct.

#spons: new release screening on PRESENT screen in 7_mins.

toy321: ATTENTION! ATTENTION! admin plans to ban my flipstream goggles. no reason given.

aria: wants opinions: lilac or sea foam?

No word about the dummy suicide. I couldn't believe Tesla was starting to get legal hassles for her latest invention, but that was kind of why I subscribed to her stream. Her drama was always the realest.

Mikey was in the Park. I continued past the Pit and thumbed in my update.

kidzero: is not living up to her potential.

I laughed, even though Mikey was probably the only one who would get my joke. I wrote to him.

kidzero: did you sign us up for studio time? @MIKEY

A minute later, he buzzed.

mikes: oops. @KID

mikes: got a frustration-high in the Park @KID

I sighed and replied.

kidzero: is coming to intervene @MIKEY

The Park was a giant playground for adrenaline junkies, and Mikey definitely had a problem. Actually, it was a problem everyone in the Game had to some degree. The designers of the Game had manufactured just the right conditions to create maximum motivation in players. They programmed the system so that each of its learning tasks engaged our present level of abilities and developed new skills in the process that were needed to take on the challenge of the next task. Always managing to hit that sweet spot between boredom and frustration to keep the obsessive freak in all of us coming back for more. There were times I'd just get lost in a mission, spending hours playing it again and again and not even realize how much progress I had made.

Yeah, it was addictive. But sweet Google, it was FUN.

The Park was located in the far corner of the first floor. It looked as if the dead department store had been possessed by a carnival, and risen up to claim the bodies of restless souls who wanted to see if they could die twice.

There was a climbing wall with varying levels of difficulty, giant trampolines, a bike racetrack, bungee Velcro walls, and a million other fun-filled ways to break your bones.

Mikey was one of the chaos of kids popping tricks off the ramps, weaving along the concrete curves of the skate park. The clatter of lost boards, the cheers and hollers of kids nailing their tricks all echoed in the space. I leaned against a wall and watched Mikey attempt his trick for the forty-seventh time.

He failed spectacularly.

I cheered him on from behind the railing, not like a supersized jerk. For real. I knew he would get it . . . eventually.

"I almost got it," he called back at me, rubbing his wrist

and kicking off again.

Mikey had a high tolerance for frustration. Some people would think it was unwise or insane to keep banging one's head against the same wall again and again, but I thought it was admirable. Talent or skill wasn't how you recognized a genius. A genius was the person giving the world the eff-you salute while doing the impossible. Mikey's scores were low, but, technically, he was probably the best player in the Game. No one could beat his raw determination.

But still. I couldn't just stand there and watch him wound himself. I absentmindedly started messing around with the piece of balloon again, wondering how I could find out more about what that stunt was all about. I amused myself by pulling and stretching it out, changing the expression of the ink lines with a tug here or there.

I worked out a way to fasten the balloon scrap to my wristband, honoring the dead dummy with a kind of mourning band. *We will not forget.*

Mikey was still trying and failing, so I turned to check out what else was happening in the Park. It was the usual anthill insanity of kids waiting restlessly in lines to get on rides or play the most physical of sports. The scoreboard showed the "Times to Beat" for the bike races and lap swimming and waterslide.

I found myself watching one guy make his way through the crowd. The crowd itself seemed to notice him too. People quit shoving and turned to watch when he passed. He was saying something to each of them, whispering to kids waiting in line to get on the trampoline or get a spot on the SlingShot. I wondered what he'd told them, because it left them staring after him. Maybe that's what I noticed, not the guy himself, but the reaction in the people around him.

He must be branded. I'd never seen him before, but cool hunters should have been all over him with his ability to shift a crowd like that.

He wasn't particularly attractive, or at least not my type. He had a genuine dread mullet—as opposed to the more common ironic dread mullet—and pretty mean-looking muscles. His cheekbones and the straight line of his nose led my eyes directly to his and trapped them there.

There was something about him. I couldn't figure it out.

As he came closer, I heard what he was telling people: "You're in . . . you're out . . . no, sorry . . . cut, uh-uh . . . out."

What was that supposed to mean? I noticed he was heading in my direction and started to feel irrationally nervous. By the time I finally made the decision to leave, it was too late.

He stopped in front of me, blocking my escape. He was wearing a climbing harness strapped over his clothes, which Ari said was a really grab accessory for Urban Climbers right now.

I looked up into his dark eyes, not saying a word. This was probably stupid, but I was holding my breath. I wanted to know if this total stranger thought I was in or out. I wanted to know what he saw when he looked at me.

"So?" I asked, ready for whatever he was going to say.

His eyes flicked down to my rubber-face-man wristband. He nodded twice, almost smiling.

"Yeah, you're in," he said quietly, leaning in close. His voice shook me like an intouch® vibration.

Then he walked on. I watched him go.

"What did he say to you?" Mikey said from behind, startling me. He was still sweaty from the skate park, his board tucked under his arm.

"Nothing," I mumbled. It was kind of embarrassing how special it made me feel that I'd made the cut for . . . whatever it was he was recruiting people for.

"Hey," Mikey said, shoving my shoulder playfully. "Did you hear the championship War Game's on for next Sunday?"

I shook my head. "Who's playing?"

"Save the Princess versus Meat Hammer."

I gagged. "Meat Hammer sounds so gross. Couldn't they think of a better team name? Was One-Eyed Flesh Spear taken?"

"Yeah, well. I told Swift I'd be there. He's playing wingman for Meat Hammer. And this is the game to see which team goes on to the league championship."

The War Gamers had been fighting for Team Player status for the last two years. Now that simulated interactive computer war games had a national tournament, they were starting to get credit. The players formed four-man (or -woman) platoons and were supposed to use communication, strategy, and wicked sniper skills to defeat the enemy.

There was this whole big debate over whether war games were too violent to be in the curriculum, but the administrators concluded that it was no more detrimental than football, so whatever. To cover collective ass, players were required to take empathy exams and psychological tests every so often to make sure that no one was getting vred and losing touch with reality.

"Wait, so Save the Princess could have a shot at going national?" I asked. Save the Princess was the only all-girl team in school. There were a few teams with the token female player, but it was predominantly a boys' club . . . thus the popularity of names like Meat Hammer and, I don't know, Man Muscle.

"Yeah, the girlies are taking names, kicking ass. You wanna join up? I hear they're recruiting for next season."

"Yeah, right."

Mikey grinned evilly. "I forgot. You can barely handle single-player games. How many friends do you have on Network now, anyway?"

"Shut up." I said, shoving him hard. But he was right, I wasn't much of a Team Player, not really into organized sports at all.

I wasn't a total social retard, I just liked keeping my friendships close and manageable. And I actually loved playing with other people despite what my Network status said.

The compositions Mikey and Ari and I worked on together were so, so different than what I'd do by myself, and if I got to choose, I'd pick collaborating with them every time. I liked that indefinable thing that happened *between* people. The connection.

My intouch® buzzed in my pocket. I looked at it.

aria: is devastated that no one's helping her choose.

I thumbed a reply immediately.

kidzero: deciding what to play at rehearsals? @ARI

Ari was our official analog instrument specialist. Her parents had given her lessons for every possible classical instrument when she was playing Level 8–12. Piano, flute, violin. She could probably single-handedly play parts for an entire geek orchestra, but she would rather be in an *Idol* band winning votes and fame. It was starting to become obvious, of the painful sort, that we didn't have the same ambitions when it came to the band.

aria: please. i'm serious. come to 4, beeotch @KID

"It's Ari," I said, putting it back into my pocket. "She's having a crisis of decision."

"Sweet Google, that girl's been getting on my twitchy last nerve."

I shrugged. "She's cliqued now, that's all."

"Yeah, OK. But that doesn't mean everything has to be such a show."

"Yeah, I know."

"Doesn't it bother you?"

"Yes, it fills me with teen angst."

We both laughed in that wincing sort of way you have to when the truth hurts. I didn't mind that Ari was so involved with the Craftsters, I just wished she wasn't always a no-show for our band practices. I told Mikey I'd let him know if I could book some Studio time and went to see what the little drama queen wanted.

4 CLIQUED

Ari had practically supernovaed when she got cliqued a few months ago.

All last season, Ari, me, and some other clique-hopefuls would go to the Sweatshop to orbit around the tight group of Craftsters. Ari did everything she could to impress Rocket, the unofficial leader of the Craftsters. Some of the girls, like Tesla Toyer, had some really inspiring projects, but I knew I didn't really fit in with their style. I tried to be a part of the scene only because it was important to Ari.

I mostly just sat to the side, gluing beads to random things—a Poke cola® can, a mic stand, a mannequin head—until, after hours and hours of mind-numbing work, they looked exactly the same, except glittery. The other girls admired them with that false-high tone of voice. "Ooh, that's . . . um, *quirky*." But it was clear that they thought my projects required a lot more insanity than skill.

They wanted someone cooler, someone with a hunger for underground fashion, someone with crazy resourceful style.

They wanted Ari.

I stood outside the Sweatshop and swiped my card at the door on the fourth floor where punk-vogue mannequins posed in the windows, and instinctively tried to fix my hair before the little light turned green. Unlike some of the other doors in the Game, this one didn't need any prerequisites to get in. It was an open workshop that just logged the hours spent inside. The time spent was divided by completed projects and input into some complicated algorithm in the Game system, which translated it all to "skill" on your record. I learned the most from open workshop studies. I preferred my activities more hands-on than on-screen.

Still, I think they probably should've had *some* kind of requirement for getting inside the Sweatshop, like superhuman self-confidence or Kevlar-tough skin. It could get vicious in there.

The Sweatshop was a weird war zone for the fashion extremist cliques. It was where the Craftsters and the Fashion Fascists held their effed-up turf wars and backstabbing beauty contests. They had catfights over who copied whose trends. Sometimes it was hard to tell the difference between the two cliques just by looking. OK, the price tags on the Fashion Fascists' straight-from-the-runway looks were insane compared to thrift-inspired finds of the Craft-sters' DIY dynamic, but they had a lot more in common with one another than they had with unfashionably normal people . . . like me.

Girls usually traveled in packs, armed with perfect hair and makeup, bulletproof smiles, and fully color-coordinated outfits. Their whole identities based on whether they claimed *craft* or *couture*.

I was entering the battle zone defenseless.

Some Fashion Fascists started mad-dogging me direct when I stepped in. Like I needed their dirty looks to know my sloppy boywear and unruly, liver-colored hair weren't scoring any points with the judges. Quelly must've texted something to the others, because their intouches® buzzed like hornets and they pointed at my pants and laughed.

I had a bright orange shoelace with one end tied to my belt loop and the other tied to my keycards or whatever. It kept things that were supposed to be in my pocket *in my pocket*, because any little thing that could get lost, I would lose.

I hurried over to where the Craftsters and their entourage were gathered. They had taken control of the airwaves and were deejaying their own anthems and choreographing rou-tines to the songs. It was probably why the Fascists looked so pissy. They couldn't play their Runway Rhythms or Trendy Pop. But honestly, I couldn't tell the difference since the

Craftsters were spinning Parody Pop at full volume.

I didn't really get the Parody Pop music trend. If the Craftsters were dissatisfied with the mainstream music selection, why didn't they play something that sounded completely different? Sometimes I wondered if the Fashion Fascists were right when they claimed that the Craftsters were just unbranded knockoffs. Ari would drop-kick me so hard if she heard me say that, though.

I squeezed past some Craftster-wannabes who were writing up some kind of manifesto for *Access to Accessories*. I glanced at one of their photo-reproed flyers. They were calling for action to reclaim the symbol of the handbag back from high-priced designers. I raised my fist in sarcastic solidarity and wondered when the *"purse-inal"* became political.

Tesla waved me over to where she sat cross-legged at a table with Ari. Tesla had been a Craftster almost since she started the Game. She had that kind of effortless self-confidence people who are naturally talented seem to have. Her blond hair was twisted up into little knots all over her head, held in place with industrial-looking bolts. If she had been less attractive, people would call her *weird*, but since she was practically gorgeous, everyone talked about her unique style.

"Hey, Kid," Tesla said, looking up from her project.

Ari sat clicking in her notebook®. She didn't look up.

"Hey, Tess," I said, sitting beside Ari. "What's going on with your flipstreams? I heard they were banned. That's . . . can the administrators even do that?"

"I don't know!" she said, more excited than concerned. "But you can buy tickets to watch the fight. You *know* I'm going to challenge their choice."

Honestly though, I wasn't surprised that the administrators had a problem with her flipstream goggles. She got the idea for them from the Making Sense area sponsored mostly by pharmaceutical companies on the third floor. She saw something about psychologists who developed a way to study the brain's response to inverted stimulus. They had people wear these glasses that flipped their vision, then made them do a bunch of tests to find out how long it took the brain to learn how to function in an upside-down world.

Tesla thought it was a cool idea but that the glasses were ugly, so she designed these sleek, streamlined strap-on shades, and they became this total grab item at school because they looked hot and completely glitched your mind. And if you had them on for too long, then you got flipped twice as hard when you took them off, because your brain needed to relearn the world again. So kids were like stumbling drunk through the passages waiting for their brains to flip back.

I was also not surprised that Tesla was all revved-up to take on the administrators. She loved a challenge, any kind of challenge. That was what made her such a mad-scientist inventor and ruthless War Game soldier.

"Mikey told me Save the Princess is playing this weekend," I said, seeing a message on my intouch® from him saying he was going to meet Swift in the Arcade. "He said it'll be . . . big. Huge. Like championship life-defining. You nervous?"

"Tesla's never nervous!" Kasi Mohindra shouted from over by the stereo. She was Save the Princess's wing-woman. "Tesla is a stone-cold killah."

Tesla smiled. "We'll be ready. Elle has us practicing non-stop until we can blast enemy faces off in our sleep. She's an amazing team captain."

"Good game," I said, smiling. "That's cool." I looked at Ari. "You going to go?"

Ari wasn't listening; she was distracted by a more high-priority concern. "What's more flattering to my skin tone, lilac or sea foam?"

"Um . . . ," I said, not knowing how to respond.

Ari launched into this monologue about a girl she spied outside of Blinded by Science. Apparently, this girl had some really grab contact lenses that made her eyes the color of gold.

"She looked so amazing! Like Palmer Phillips!" Ari went on.

I thought for a second about the color of little Lexie Phillips's eyes. Was it genetics or a family-pack of those fake-eye contacts that made her eyes the exact same shade as her brother's?

Rocket sighed. "Everything about Palmer is pure gold." She pulled out her intouch®, probably to text her affections.

Ari was still talking: "And she was telling me about all the different colors they have, and that I can get them prescription, and where to get them, and I *want* them. Now help me think of a way to get my mom to buy them for me."

"I like your eyes," I said. They were a pretty hazelnut color.

Ari looked at me, offended. "Poo brown? Are you kidding me? Come on, think! You need to HELP ME. What if I lost my contacts like I lost my glasses? That would work again, right?"

"Uh, why don't you just ask your mom? She gives you anything you want anyway," I mumbled. Ari's mom was so cool—she understood the direct correlation between getting new shit and getting popularity points. Not like my mom, who'd totally be like, *WTF? No.*

"I know, she's so lame," Ari said, rolling her eyes. "I mean, put up a fight, woman! How am I going to hone my powers of persuasion if she gives in so easily?"

The other Craftsters laughed. The topic was re: moms ruining our lives and not re: anything I might want to talk about.

I didn't even know why Ari was stressing about eye color. Her light brown hair was cut chin-length, with bangs grown to be fashionably too long. They fell just below her eyes, hiding them from everybody.

So I sat there, depping about not being heard, while Ari comparison-shopped lilac vs. sea foam. "I swear you guys want to see me fail," Ari said, pulling out her intouch®. "I'm gonna ask Jaye. If I were branded, this would so not be an issue."

She was probably right. If Ari were branded, she'd only have to mention she was interested, and she would just get it. Anything she wanted. I mean, look at Rocket. Only branded three weeks and already stitching PROPERTY OF PALMER PHILLIPS on her underwear. That was a joke, by the way. None of the Craftsters thought it was funny when I told it to them, either.

Ari curled over her intouch® to text her advisor, and I opened up my notebook® to see if there were any Network announcements.

"Hey, that's crafty," Rocket said, grabbing my wrist. "Did you make it?"

"Sort of," I said and briefly mentioned the scene in the Pit. The bore-core dummy's belly flop into the uncaring crowd below.

"Huh, I hadn't heard about that," Rocket said, pulling her long dark hair back into an effortlessly sophisticated twist. "Anyone else see it?"

"Yeah! I was totally there! I saw the whole thing!" Ari answered enthusiastically.

"Oh," Rocket said. "Well, what did the sweater look like? I want to knit one. It's going to be so cult."

Ari tried to describe the sweater, the scratchy-looking drab-green wool, the puke-colored elbow patches. I just kept on seeing the silhouettes moving up on the fifth floor. My stomach clenched again when I remembered the sight of the falling body.

"Hold on, maybe someone posted images. Let me use

your notebook®, Kid. I don't want to clear my eyewear searches."

Ari swiveled my notebook® over to her before I could answer and started to do a search.

"What did the sign say?" Ari asked.

"'Choose your suicide,'" I mumbled, moving in behind Ari to see the screen.

"OK."

She did a product search for *Choose your suicide*.

"Ew."

"Gross," Ari announced so everyone would come look. "That is so not right."

The search pulled up a lot of unpleasant snuff images, crime scene photos, and charts showing the comparative effectiveness of various methods of doing the deed, but no relevant hits.

Everyone huddled to look at the screen now. Avery used her wide hip to bump Tesla out of the way.

"Hey, that's pretty cheap," Avery said, pointing to an advertisement on the screen.

"You're so sick." Kasi laughed.

"What? I'm just saying that's a really good deal on razor blades and sleeping pills."

"Uh, can we focus here?" Ari said, clearing the search, obviously enjoying the attention.

"Try 'Unidentified,'" I said, remembering the first part of the sign.

She typed in *Unidentified*.

And a video came up.

A close-up of an inflated red balloon face filled the screen. We were seeing the dummy victim before the fall. The soundtrack was soft and haunting, an almost familiar melody. The simple zombie-bored expression, drawn in black Sharpie on the inflated balloon, stared out from the screen.

When the camera zoomed out, you could see the dummy propped up against the railing where I saw it drop, just outside of the Arcade on the fifth floor. The dummy stood there alone, in its green sweater and ill-fitting pants, looking down into the Pit.

The music-box tones changed into screeching white noise, with a heavy rhythmic thump. A kind of chest bone–rattling adrenal bass bumping, an oddly authentic representation of how I felt actually being there.

Once again, the body fell. Super–slow motion and over the noise music, a voice:

"We are the Unidentified. The Unidentified refuses to be typecast, target-marketed, corporate-identified, defined."

The body had reached the ground by now; the picture cut to another angle as the balloon burst in real time. Someone in the crowd had been filming.

"Your identity is reduced with every choice you fake, with every secret they take. . . . They make an offer and you buy it. Things you are told are freedoms in fact limit your choices. You

hold a razor blade to your soul. You choose your suicide."

The camera panned across the crowd looking at the body. On the screen, I saw myself. I saw my not-so-well-disguised panic, how I turned away from the body, and looked at Ari.

It was surreal.

The video finished with the words, *"We refuse to choose our suicide."*

Everyone sat there quietly for a moment.

Then Rocket asked, "So do you think this green would work?" She held up a skein of yarn.

"I saw a beige in the basket over there that could work for the elbow patches," Ari said helpfully.

That was all they had to say?

"So was that supposed to be a kind of protest?" I blurted out.

"What do you mean?" Kasi said, distracted.

"I don't know. That message seemed really antisponsor, don't you think?"

"Yeah, I guess," Rocket said.

"'The Unidentified.' I don't get it," Avery said, leaning back on the sofa. "What's wrong with having an identity? About liking what you like?"

"I know, right? How can they be, like, antichoices?" one of the Craftster-wannabes piped up, ready to voice her opinion now that she knew what everyone else thought. "They're, like, enemies to democracy or something."

"Oh, come on," I said. "Aren't the Craftsters supposed

44

to be against consumer culture, too? All that handmade, DIY, fight-the-Fascists stuff?"

I looked over at Avery, the diamond-studded image of Che Guevara on her red T-shirt stretched wide across her sizable breasts. She rolled her eyes.

"I'm not defending what they did, I'm just trying to understand—"

"Kid . . ." Ari began, but then just shook the hair out of her face and sighed dramatically.

No one was going to say I was wrong, but everyone seemed to think I needed to shut up. I guess that's why I wasn't Miss Popularity or even Miss Congeniality. I was like the runner-up to Miss Mediocrity, and my prize was awkward silence.

The Fashion Fascists decided to use the distraction of my social suicide to execute a raid on the *Flirt16* magazines and a bitch fest broke out.

"Hey! I was looking at that, you slut," Avery called after them. Avery was always ready for a fight.

"Right, like you could ever pull off that look with all that junk in your trunk," Quelly sniped.

"She's, like, smuggling cottage cheese."

The Fascists shrieked with laughter as they carried the yoinked look-books back to their side of the room.

"Like, ten pounds of the generic store-brand stuff!" Ashleah Carter called out.

The Craftsters huddled in around Avery to plan retaliatory attacks. It involved arming themselves with lipstick and covertly marking the backs of Fascists' skirts and jeans in strategic areas.

I was just about to close my notebook® and clear out before metaphorical blood was shed, but first I linked to the Unidentified film from my page. I wanted Mikey to see this, and I trusted him to show the apropriate amount of curiosity for the stunt.

Besides, Winterson just told me I needed to start showing more interests on Network, and this was the most interesting thing I'd ever seen happen in the Game.

5 WIRED

I left the Sweatshop feeling . . . I didn't know. I felt more like a sound, hollow like wind whooshing. I pulled out my intouch® and thumbed in:

kidzero: is free-falling. catch me.

It was always so much easier to know what I was feeling when I had to put it into words, or more accurately, under one hundred characters, and send it off into the world.

The Unidentified video was still bugging me. Or maybe it wasn't even the video, maybe it was the response to the video that bugged me. The lack of response. People in school were tossing bodies over the edge and no one cared enough to figure out why.

I watched my message get pushed to the bottom of the tiny screen by all the incoming sponsor messages. It made me feel better. How could a person stumble down into an empty void when the place was filled with so much fun stuff?

#spons: the Studio is available for sign-up.

The Studio, part of the music center, was on the other end of the fourth floor. I started down the hall still cradling my purring intouch® and put out a call to Mikey.

kidzero: what doing? @MIKEY

Judging by his reply, Mikey was playing a simulation game in the Arcade.

mikes: is collapsing the global economy. wee!

This was followed quickly by a comment from Jeremy Swift.

swiftx: is annoyed by incompetent day traders @MIKEY

I laughed and got in on the discussion.

kidzero: ha! swift thinks you're a merchant banker=wanker @MIKEY

Then I immediately felt like I got caught looking. It was so rude to reply to personal conversations like that. But I was probably safe; Jeremy wouldn't be able to see my comment unless I directed it @ him, or if he was following my stream. And I seriously doubted Jeremy Swift would ever subscribe to my stream.

I didn't follow too many streams, just the few friends I had on Network. I followed Swift's because he was a friend of Mikey's, otherwise he was completely out of my social orbit. He had like three thousand friends because he was branded and a big-shot War Gamer and seminotorious Crackhead programmer. I had like eleven. Pathetic, but true.

The fact that Swift just shouted out Mikey in his stream was probably going to result in a surge of subscribers to Mikey's stream. Now that I commented on their convo, Mikey probably thought I was one of Swift's stream-groupies too.

Stream-groupies subscribed to all the high-score players and branded kids' streams to get in on the gossip flow. Ari was a total stream-groupie. I didn't know how she did it. I could barely keep up with the handful of friends I follow, and the #spons messages, *and* the Game PLAYs.

Besides, it didn't feel right to clutter up my intouch® with the opinions of people like Eva Bloom or Palmer Phillips. I really didn't care what they thought, even if they were branded.

I was starting to angst about buttoning into the convo when Mikey responded.

mikes: we're playing buy sell & destroy on 5! come! @KID

I smiled and continued up the escalator. To my surprise, Jeremy replied.

swiftx: who're you talking to? @MIKEY

Now it was painfully obvious that he wasn't subscribed to my stream. I felt so invisible.

mikes: kid. @SWIFT

swiftx: yeah, come log him off b4 he crashes banking system @KID

My breath kind of caught in my throat. Jeremy Swift sent a reply directly to *me*. I imagined that my intouch® purred louder when he wrote to me, that the weight of his popularity shook my machine more.

Just as I got to the entrance of the Arcade, my intouch® chirped. It meant that I got a new PLAY clue, an assignment I needed to do for Game score.

PLAY: In what year did paper cease to be produced from tree pulp? text back before close of Game for time bonus.

I hesitated for a nanosecond. I thought it must have been a trick question. Everyone knew paper was made from a reusable plastic resin, printed ink washed from it with a chemical solution and saved for a new print run. A paper made from trees? That must've been back in the Wood Ages.

I usually jumped on all the Game clues to get the time bonuses, but I wasn't even sure which floor I needed to explore to find the answer to this one, and . . . I really couldn't even fake an interest in USian history right now. Mikey wanted me in the Arcade. And so did Swift?

I swiped my card at the entrance to the Arcade and went in. All the strobe glows of hundreds of screens flashed strange shadows on the dark, cavelike walls. I listened to the hushed music of the Arcade. The tinny sound of explosions escaping through headsets. A symphony of trigger-clicking, button tapping . . . crescendoing into an outburst of expletive, a cry of triumph. Kids sat across from one another in these long rows of desks, with LCD monitors stretched down the middle. But the monitors blocked the view of the other person, and reflected back a window into their own private virtual worlds.

There were no available ports, so I was put in the queue. I went over to the Tech Support Desk to see how long the wait was. Elle Rodriguez, the Save the Princess team captain, was manning the desk. She was typing ridiculously fast, her silver-painted fingernails flashing. The text on her screen reflected in her pink-tinted glare-resistant glasses.

She saw me and smiled. "Hey, you're Tesla's friend, right?—Kid, hi—Problems logging on?—The server's got attitude today—Oh, you're on standby, cool—Something should open up soon, or I could bump this perv, he's been on since we opened—Whoa! You've got, like, three weeks worth of hours stored up!—Don't tell anyone, but there's a black market for excess hours. You could make bank."

She had already accessed my account information and found the answers to her questions before I could give them. She talked as fast as she typed.

I just stood there kind of dazed as she started to ramble on about the protocol of hours auctions and the zen of troubleshooting.

"How do you even have so many hours saved up? What're you, a monk?" Elle laughed.

I just shrugged. No one ever really understood when I told them I wasn't interested in staring into screens, especially not the SimKids who hung out in the Arcade, so I'd given up trying to explain it. Not that I really knew how to explain it. I just felt like I needed to spend my time doing something real.

Mikey bounced up and practically tackled me from behind.

"You can squeeze in with me and Swift," he said, out of breath.

I scanned the room looking for Jeremy's mop of dark hair. He was staring intensely at a screen, his broad shoulders tense beneath his trademark black T-shirt. A small crowd of point-gawkers gathered behind him, watching him play.

"Hey, are you guys coming to the War Game?" Elle asked.

"We'll be there."

"Awesome." She looked at Mikey, and squinted. "You're a meatpounder, aren't you?"

I laughed. Mikey looked horrified.

"No! I . . . I like girls."

"I'm just messing with you. Swift's a friend of mine, too. It's going to be a great game."

We waved good-bye and left her desk.

"I think she likes you," I teased Mikey.

His ears turned red. It wasn't outside of the realm of possibility that a girl like Elle would hit on Mikey. If you didn't mind your guys being made up entirely of elbows and Adam's apples, Mikey was pretty cute.

"Not interested," he mumbled.

"Come on, she wants your meat."

It looked like he was preparing a witty comeback, but the time for that had already passed.

I just laughed at him, and we walked over to Jeremy and his entourage. The girls hovering over his shoulder glared at me as I squeezed in beside Mikey, who reclaimed the empty seat by Jeremy.

"What are you guys playing?" I asked, looking at Mikey's screen.

"Jeremy cracked a version of Buy, Sell & Destroy. It's this game where you're a hot-shit investment banker that goes around crippling economies, exploiting disaster, and projecting profits, all while snorting lines of credit and living luxe. Wanna play?"

I just said, "Nah, I'm not interested in finance."

"You're not supposed to cripple economies," Jeremy mumbled. "You're supposed to make profits. You start out as a trader in the pit at the New York Stock Exchange. Then you build up your fortune and work your way up the financial ladder with speculative investments, innovative schemes, and backroom dealings without getting caught."

"What's that?" I asked, pointing to a pulsing ball in the corner of the screen.

"It's a kind of stress meter," Mikey said. "You can get an ulcer, heart attack, or aneurysm if you don't watch it. Bills pile up, demands from your wife, criminal investigations into your firm, all this stuff adds stress."

I looked at Mikey's stress meter. It looked pink and happy.

"You don't seem too stressed-out."

"Nah, I don't give a shit." Mikey laughed and made his avatar try to climb out of the Pit.

I looked back to Jeremy's screen. His stress meter was ballooning.

"Ah! Look out! Your stress levels are going from like red to purple? It looks . . . bad."

"Yeah," Jeremy said, flicking his eyes to me for a millisecond. "But it's OK, my shift is almost done. After work, I'll get drunk and boink an intern. It's the fastest way to reduce stress."

"That's effed up," I said. The girls behind Jeremy giggled nervously.

"Mikey!" Jeremy yelled. "Learn to play or log out of the game! Your renegade trading is making investors lose confidence in the system."

"I know how to play," Mikey said, clicking absentmindedly on a button.

"What did you do?" Jeremy snapped.

"What? Nothing."

"Mikey! What did you *do*?"

"I just sold all my stocks."

"Well, stop it. You're causing a panic. Now everyone's dropping their stocks. This is the cracked interactive version, and you're effing up my game! Do you know how long it took me to inflate the value on those stocks?"

"This is boring," Mikey complained.

I watched Jeremy, his attention still focused on the game. He bit his lip and squinted his eyes. I felt a little thrill to be this close to him.

I daydreamed for a moment, imagining him being as interested in me as he was in the game. Then I noticed Mikey staring at me, and felt like I just got caught looking at puppy porn.

I attempted to cover up my embarrassment by searching through my bag, wishing I could crawl inside it.

"Mikey, shit," I said, remembering something he'd find more interesting than my awkward infatuation. "There's something I wanted to show you." I took my notebook® out of my bag and opened it. "Did you see this?"

I pulled up the Unidentified film from my page and played it for him.

The people who had been watching the legendary Swift play video games gathered behind me to peek at the film too. I wondered how Jeremy could stand people hovering around him like that.

I glanced back at Jeremy. I caught him looking at me. His rain-cloudy eyes seemed to see me for the first time. It made me hyper-self-conscious.

I turned back to the film.

Mikey frowned, still watching the screen. He watched the splatter. The crowd shot. Me on-screen.

"That was kind of intense," Mikey said at last. "Are you OK? How was it . . . you know, being there?"

Mikey really surprised me sometimes. He could be totally, completely, stupidly insensitive, but then he could be the *most* sensitive. He was the only one who ever asked me how I felt and actually seemed to care about the answer.

"I'm OK. It wasn't real."

He looked back at the screen. "Yeah, but I bet it felt real."

6 LOOK AND LISTEN

Mikey and me logged out of the Arcade and squinted at the light streaming in from the skylight. The sky felt so close when you were up here on the fifth floor. We leaned against the railing where the dummy had been pushed.

"I can't believe someone would be vred enough to drop a body in the middle of the Game," Mikey said, looking down into the Pit, leaning over the railing a little. He stood on one foot, stretched his arms out, ready for a Superman *whoosh* into the air below. "You think they'll get caught?"

"I saw who did it," I blurted out.

"Wow, you're terrible at this. You're supposed to build up suspense before the reveal. I know your Media Literacy scores are low, but I thought you'd at least—"

"I'm not playing. I saw them."

"What?"

"Well, I didn't see who it was, but I saw them do it. There were two of them, or maybe more, now I don't remember what I saw."

Mikey was quiet for a moment, then he said, "I can't believe you actually saw it happen. I'm so jealous."

"What do you mean?"

"How often is there a glitch in the Game? When something completely unprogrammed and unexpected happens?"

"Ari thought the sponsors did it," I said. "And the Craftsters were more interested in the look than the action."

"Your friends lack imagination," Mikey joked. "There's no way the sponsors came up with it."

"How do you know?" I asked, but I already knew the answer too. I knew it from the second I saw the body tip over the edge. I felt it. The ache of an authentic moment. The real thing.

"The sponsors can only *wish* they could come up with something that cool." Mikey laughed.

"Did you see my souvenir?" I said, holding up my balloon-face wristwatch.

"Good game," he said. "But is it wise to walk around with crime-scene evidence strapped to your arm?"

Could I get in trouble for picking up a piece of trash? Was anyone even looking for who was responsible? I mean, besides us.

"Look," I said, pointing up at the telltale spy boxes, red recording lights lazily blinking. "Looks like whoever did it is not going to get caught. At least, not caught on film."

All the old surveillance cameras, reminders of the building's less-tech life as a mall, had been posed and repositioned in new angles. Instead of focusing on the passages and the Pit, they were pointing at each other in playfully paranoid staring contests.

I never really noticed the cameras before. They had always been part of the architecture, background scenery, but now it looked like they were creating some center-stage drama.

Two cameras in particular were angled toward each other so delicately that they almost looked intimate. Like lovers sharing a secret, whispering that they only had eyes for each other.

"Cute," I said and took an intouch® snapshot of the private moment. There was something so creepy-sweet about it. Surveillance cameras in love. Stalker romance. "You want to see if there's still time available in the Studio?" I asked Mikey while saving the photo.

I was playing back the drum track Mikey had just laid down. He was so good. I'd told him about the bird-wing beats I'd noticed in the Pit, and he captured the syncopated speed perfectly. It was just a snare drum rhythm, but it flew forward in my headphones. I listened not only to what we had recorded, but to the sounds that were missing. The sounds I needed to find to make the song complete.

Mr. Levy tapped on the glass, and I took the headphones off.

"Closing time, Kid," he said.

"Oh, yeah. OK," I said, looking at my intouch®. I couldn't believe it was already almost five o'clock. I backed up the drum track and got my stuff.

"I already had to chase Williams out of here," Mr. Levy said. I craned my neck, hoping to get a glimpse of Tycho Williams. He was branded, but I swear I wasn't a gawker. I just had always been really impressed by the music he made.

"What're you working on?" Mr. Levy asked.

"Just a new track with Mikey."

Mr. Levy looked back into the Studio. "Where is he?"

I shrugged. Mikey had left after recording. He liked the energy of playing, but lost interest when I started geek-listening on repeat. I could play it back over and over and never get bored, but Mikey says that was because I was hearing stuff that wasn't there.

Mr. Levy was checking the other soundproof booths. I was the last one left again. "Whatever happened to that one track I heard . . . the ambient-room composition?"

"It's not finished," I mumbled. It was a music project I called *Background Checks*, and it made me uncomfortable that Mr. Levy had heard parts of it before it was complete.

He waited for me to log out of the Studio, then checked his player records to make sure everyone had logged out.

"Your songs are getting a lot of play at the Listening

Library, Kid," he said, lowering the clanking metal grate over the storefront. "Even though your constant name changes don't make your uploaded tracks easy to find."

I shrugged. "We can't decide on what we want to call ourselves." Mikey, Ari, and me often added our silly fool-around sorta-songs to the Library, releasing each track under a different band name. It made our songs unsearchable by artist, but coming up with inappropriate band names was half the fun of making music.

"But it speaks to the quality of sound you're producing that your tracks are getting multiple listens despite no name recognition," he continued.

"Oh, I haven't been checking rankings," I mumbled.

"Murdoch West from the Hit List has been asking me about new talent," he said. "They're looking for artists to promote. If you just played your stuff for them, you—"

"I'm going to miss the shuttle. See you tomorrow, Mr. Levy," I said, making my escape toward the escalator.

I didn't like the way Mr. Levy was singling me out. I wasn't interested in getting our songs on the Hit List—I just wanted to play with my friends.

7 LOGGED OUT

My head felt kind of cloudy as I held up my ID and walked through the doors, exiting the Game.

The parking lot was almost completely empty. I'd missed Ari's text that she was leaving if I needed a ride, and the last Game shuttle to my neighborhood was about to leave.

Mom was going to be pissed if I missed the shuttle. She couldn't afford to take time off work to pick me up and would probably have to ask Aunt Gillie to get me. Of course, she could just authorize my Game card to allow me to take the metro. But she wouldn't. She thought it was unsafe.

Mom was one of the millions of overprotective parents who loved the fact that players in the Game got intouches® with GPS tracking.

I took a seat on the shuttle, listening again to Mikey's wing beats on my headphones. I thought about this morning in the Pit, the bird fight, the body drop, the soundtrack to the Unidentified film. Music box and white noise and bird wings.

I stared out the window and watched sunlight flash off parked cars in even bursts, almost like trumpet blasts. I wondered if I could get Ari to play trumpet, or maybe clarinet bird squawks were what this track needed.

I thought of Ari. Ari's eyes. *Poo-brown eyes,* she said. She wanted me to help her choose. *Things you think are freedoms really limit your choices,* who said that? Lilac eyes. Sea foam eyes. Out the window. Eyes are the windows to the soul. Razor blade to your soul. *Choose your suicide. We refuse to choose our suicide.*

I took my headphones off, and shook my head.

My intouch® purred in my bag and I dug it out.

aria: what doing? @KID

I wasn't supposed to text after I logged out of the Game because the wireless charges after closing time were insane. Mom freaked out when she got the bill after the first season. She had overlooked the hidden costs from the local service provider of the "free" intouch® that were mentioned in the fine print agreement when she signed me up for Level 13–17.

I promised Mom I would text only in emergencies after

five. But this was Ari—this was important. So I replied.

kidzero: nothing. new track, you should hear @ARI

aria: so i saw that swift totally @ed you today! @KID

I smiled, but then got self-conscious. If Ari noticed Swift @ed my name, then a lot of people could have noticed. I might have a bunch more subscribers following this conversation than usual.

kidzero: don't have the credit to text right now @ARI

My intouch® purred again.

aria: boo. you're boring. @KID

I unlocked the front door with the keycard from my shoelace keychain.

Mom wasn't home yet, which wasn't unusual. She worked Game hours fielding customer complaints for one of the telecom sponsors, but most nights she waitressed the dinner shift at her sister's restaurant.

So I was left to forage for myself and our lazy dog, Lump, until she got home. My mom never bought the good kinds of snacks, but I had the Vending Machine in the Game to satisfy all my munching needs.

I fed the dog, and carried my bowl of semisweetened cereal to my room.

It was too quiet in my house. The silence was an itch.

I put on the music project I'd been mixing whenever Ari and Mikey punked out on band practice. *Background Checks*. I recorded and looped "amplified room hum," pulling apart ambient noise to find danceable rhythms and simple melodies.

I liked to play it when I was feeling this way, weirdly empty and uncomfortable. The quiet wasn't so lonely if you listened to how much sound was hidden in silence. The fan rattle of overheating appliances, fridge motors, and like all the tiny vibrating tones of light bulbs and neon buzzes that we barely notice but surround us every day.

I got to the part that Mr. Levy had heard, where I'd amplified the faint chirps of my intouch® recharging and layered it with a fly trying to escape out a closed window. I thought about what he'd said about the Hit List cool hunter who would probably promote it. Ari would pounce on this chance, but I didn't make this music to be an access ticket into the VIP Lounge. I don't really know *why* I made this music, but it wasn't to get me branded.

I opened my notebook®. My intouch® default settings uploaded saved images automatically to the Network, and I found myself staring at the pic of the security cameras posing for each other. What kind of people went through the trouble of doing something like that? Who were they?

I clicked to view the dummy suicide video a few times. Listened to the baritone voice say what the Unidentified wasn't, giving no clue to what they *were*.

I closed my notebook® again and let the *Background Checks* music bleed into the sounds of my own room. The heater turning on and off, trying to keep the homeostasis of warmth in the house, and the traffic from the street outside. After a while I heard the TV switched on in the other room and the volume turned up.

It was the sound of my mom coming home.

"Kiddie!" Mom called out, and I turned off my music and went to see her.

Mom was collapsed on the sofa, watching the news. She was always so exhausted; working all the time, stressing about making debt payments, and feeling guilty about not being here when I got home. I kissed the top of her head.

"Did you feed Lump?" she asked me automatically.

"Yeah."

I always fed Lump when I got home, but she always asked. I could make a big deal out of it, tell her that I didn't need her to remind me, but if she stopped one day, I would probably miss our ritual.

"I brought home some dinner," she said, gesturing to a bag of restaurant leftovers on the table. I scavenged through the containers, happy to have some real-looking food.

"How was it tonight?" I said, helping myself to Aunt Gillie's famous macaroni and cheese.

"Slow," she said with the same tone she would've used if

she had said "busy." She hated it when it was slow because the tips were so bad it didn't even make it worth her time being there, but she hated when it was busy just as much. The tips would be decent, but she was already so tired from working the phones all day, it took the last of her energy to have to race around all night.

"Why do you keep doing shifts there? Can't Aunt Gillie find someone else to cover?" I said with my mouth full of food.

"You almost missed the shuttle today," she said, sitting up and looking at me.

I flinched. Of course, she would be checking my GPS coordinates at closing time.

"Yeah, but I didn't."

She had that look, I could tell she was playing an imaginary horror film of everything that *could have* gone wrong if I'd been stranded outside of the Game without a ride. "Where was Ari?"

"She already left. I just lost track of time."

"You need to take more responsibility for your actions," she went on. "Your mistakes don't affect just you." I'd heard this all before.

"You worry too much."

"Guess why," she said simply. She turned back to the TV that was so old that you could tell you were watching a screen.

There were more reports of so-called minor mobs. I wondered who had so-called them that. It made them sound like no big deal, but maybe that was the point.

The government had just proposed legislation to raise the legal age to twenty-one. It threatened to extend the prohibitions against underage gathering in public places on to Bonus Level campuses too, and there had been protest parties. They showed clips of law enforcement using tear gas to break up "potentially illegal gatherings" and kids just continuing to dance in their gas masks.

I watched the images on the screen. It looked like it would've been a totally harmless party if the cops weren't using brute force to try and stop it.

"I don't want you getting caught up in what's going on out there, Kiddie," Mom said, watching a girl get dragged across the dance floor by the authorities. "As soon as the Game is done, I want you on that shuttle, and I want you home."

8 TAG, YOU'RE IT

I fumbled with my ID card at the Level 13–17 entrance. The doors wheezed open and the late-morning sun blazed through the skylight. I felt like an ant under a magnifying glass.

Operating on autopilot, I turned on my intouch® and felt it seizure in my hands with all my missed messages. I hid in the shadow of one of the "trees" at the edge of the Pit to read the texts without the sun glare on the display.

I just got messages from the sponsors, and a few updates from Ari, but no shout-outs to respond to. I put my intouch® away and was about to jump down from the edge of the planter but stopped to stare at a peek of pink blooming in the black soil where the "trees" buried their roots.

Someone on the other side of the planter said the words "Illegal Arts Workshop." I perked up and tuned in on their conversation. Notice of Illegal Arts Workshops were spread entirely through word-of-mouth. They were totally unauthorized, and always a guaranteed good time.

But it wasn't just the content of the conversation that caught my attention, I couldn't stop listening to the sound of the speaker's voice. I knew it from somewhere. I turned to see who was talking, and recognized the guy from the Park the other day sitting on the opposite edge of the planter.

He was flirting with a girl who looked vaguely familiar, but I couldn't think of where I'd seen her before.

She had short black hair and a small pink circle drawn high on her cheekbone. I was still trying to figure out how I knew her, when she looked over at me. The way she was staring reminded me of the birds in the Pit, defiant and unblinking.

The Urban Climber guy with the honeybee voice turned to look at me then too. He smiled, and I should've looked away, pretended to mess around with my intouch® or something, but instead I sort of smiled back. I felt caught. That's the best word I had to explain it—captured. Captivated.

"Is there something we can help you with?" he said pleasantly, even though I'd just got caught lurking.

"Sorry," I mumbled. I grabbed my bag to leave, when I decided to just ask him. "You were in the Park the other day," I said. "You were telling everyone whether they were in or out."

"Yes," he answered, even though I didn't get a chance to ask my question.

"What were . . . How did you decide who to choose?"

The girl still hadn't said a word, but she was staring at me hard. I couldn't read her expression, and it was making me uncomfortable.

He shrugged and said, "It was completely random. How do you choose?"

Something javajacked in my memory when he spoke the word "choose." "What do you mean?"

"That's what they want to know: what's in and who's out. They monitor all our interactions, looking for a way to untangle our complicated social systems to know what string to pull. When they're watching for reasons, a random choice is the most subversive."

I thought about that for a while. I understood all the words he used, but it still felt like he was speaking another language.

I glanced quickly at the girl he was with, then said, "You told me I was in."

"Yeah, well. What do I know, right?"

He turned back to the girl with eyes like a bird, and I felt . . . disappointed.

"Kid!" I heard Ari calling my name. "Kid!"

I looked out from my corner, back into the brightness of the Pit. The sun reflected off the white tabletops, and through the glare I saw Ari. She was surrounded by a colorful flock of Craftsters. Ari waved me over and I got up to go to her.

"See you later, Kid," the guy said softly as I hurried past

71

them. I sat by Ari in the bright sun, trying to shake off the weird feeling. He made me feel like he could see my secrets, and I didn't even know his name.

"What was going on over there?" Ari asked, craning her neck to look at the shadowy corner.

"Nothing. I don't know," I said honestly, but Ari frowned like I was keeping something from her.

She turned back to the Craftsters and continued to add her voice and laughter to the chatter. I just kind of sat there, watching them flip through pages of glossy feminist magazines, their poet-rockstar hairstyles teased up like the feather displays of jungle birds.

My intouch® chirped. I had gotten a new PLAY message:

PLAY: what is the acceleration of a body in free fall? submit before noon for time bonus.

I stared at the question. I knew "body" meant "any object" in physics-talk, but the question was eerie considering what went down here yesterday. The creepy feeling that someone knew my secrets just got stronger. It couldn't be a coincidence—the administrators and sponsors must know something about that stunt, right?

I heard one of the Craftsters shriek, "Yeah! We should totally go!" followed by the goose-squawks of everyone's chairs getting pushed back at the same time.

Ari was on her feet and noticed that I was still sitting there. She looked at me, then back to the rest of the crew flocking toward the passage, chitter-chatter and perfume plumes following after them.

Rocket glanced back at Ari, "You coming?"

Ari said she was coming, but sat down beside me, grinning at me, all breathless and brilliant.

Anyway, there we were alone at last and she was like, "Hey. So, did you hear?"

"What?"

"Come on, don't *tell* me you didn't hear."

"Ari. Just say it."

Ari had been known to hype the news of what she ate for breakfast.

"Guess whose page Aerwear cool hunters have visited eight times now?"

Her uncorked-champagne thumbs popped up, pointing to her chest with all the subtlety of a neon sign.

"How do you know?"

"I've been tracking views," she said, putting her finger to her lips. "There's a script code you can just copy and paste to watch who's watching—but don't spread it around, because admin will block it if they find out." Then she squealed, "I'm totally going to get branded!"

"That's great!" I said with as much enthusiasm as I could fake.

She frowned. "You're just saying that."

"What?"

"You don't really want me to get branded."

It kind of sucked that Ari knew me so well.

"I know this is something you really, really want. And you deserve it. You've been working so hard. I will be deliriously happy for you when you get it."

Ari jumped up, flung her arms around my head, and squeezed.

I didn't really see the point of branding. What was so great about being linked to a logo? Or maybe I just cultivated this attitude because it was never going to happen to me, and it was just easier to laugh with Mikey about it than obsessing over attracting cool hunter attention like Ari did.

People who got branded enjoyed a fair amount of fame and notoriety on campus. And if Ari got her status upgraded to the It List, everyone was going to know her name. She would get access to the VIP Lounge, the gathering place for Generation Triple-A. It was the exclusive lounge where rumors were made—the rumors of the place itself were legendary. All the free stuff they get. How they get to mingle with the cool hunters and brand representatives, who listen to them because their opinions *matter* and can make a difference. Getting branded fast-tracked you into a career of media, marketing, and shaping public opinion, which was what Ari always wanted.

She checked her intouch®, then looked at me. "You are coming, right? You should COME!"

"Where?"

"To the Physics of Hollywood walkthrough in the Lecture Hall. Palmer Phillips invited Rocket and all of us to come because they're going to sneak-preview clips from

next summer's blockbusters."

Ari guilted me into following along with the other Craftsters, so I logged in to one of the scheduled Hints, Cheats, and Walkthroughs.

The lesson would probably cover some momentum and trajectory physics questions, and it would be the quickest way to solve my PLAY clue. But mostly I went to be with Ari. It felt like we weren't interested in the same stuff anymore, and I missed just being around her. I didn't need a Newtonian equation to figure out that the distance between us would increase at a ridiculous rate if we didn't spend more time together.

So we all logged in to the Lecture Hall. It was a grab lesson. Mr. Tom Rogers was debunking the physics of Hollywood; showing all the action scenes of bodies flying through glass windows, noncombustible objects bursting into flames, guys getting electrocuted, stuff like that. Then he used computer animation (he's the Digital Visual Effects instructor up on fifth) to enter in equations and apply the laws of physics to the scenes.

It was actually creepier to see the scenes with the real-world effects. Gruesome. Everyone in the Lecture Hall cringed as the carnage piled up on screen. Palmer Phillips had his arm around Rocket. She closed her eyes and hid her face in his shoulder. Palmer and some of his wiseass friends were laughing, but it was nervous laughter, the tone of it a little too sharp to be genuine.

I texted Mikey.

kidzero: what do you think about mixing recordings of laughter? @MIKEY

kidzero: it would make acoustically extreme music @MIKEY

mikes: do it. @KID

I set my intouch® to record, waiting for the nervous titters. I was feeling restless. Screens never held my attention for very long, even if they were flashing a series of crumpling bodies, and my attention started to wander. Watching the wide eyes of the audience.

I noticed someone else not paying attention. I recognized her, the girl with the bird eyes from this morning. Was she following me?

I could hardly see her face because her head was bent down, focused on her desk. She was carving something into the plastic desktop.

Her hair was shaved in the back, bowl-cut on top. It wasn't a very grab haircut, but it made clear that she wasn't trying to be pretty. Silver earrings lined the rim of her ear and I recognized the pink circle high on her cheekbone. I couldn't tell if it was makeup or paint or a tattoo or what.

There was a screech of car tires on the screen, a sickening crash, and the kids groaned. Then laughed.

But she didn't look up. The slow-burning flames from the screen reflected in her straight black hair, which swayed slightly with the effort of etching something into the desk.

Mr. Rogers gave some final hints to the class about Newton's Second Law and the forces acting on a falling object, and then the lesson was over.

I quickly thumbed in my PLAY reply: *9.8 m/s²* and hit Submit.

Ari said loudly to the Craftsters, "I swear to Google, I think I almost puked."

They all chattered in agreement, their faces lit with delighted terror.

"Did you almost puke?" Ari asked me.

I was watching the girl write on the desk.

"Did you almost puke?" she asked me again. "That was sick, right?"

I nodded, distracted. Everyone was gathering their stuff and heading toward the exit, but Palmer Phillips was walking over to the girl finishing up the etching in her desk. She looked up to see him standing there, all broad shoulders and unnaturally blond hair. She quickly picked up her stuff to leave, and he just grinned at her. I'd heard that Palmer Phillips had his right canine sharpened to start a new trend—so far the lopsided vampire look hadn't caught on.

"Ari?" I said, grabbing her arm. "Who's that? Over there with Palmer Phillips."

At the sound of Palmer's name, Ari laser-beamed her attention to that side of the room. She frowned. "That's Cayenne Lewis."

"*What?*" I nearly shrieked. "*That's* Cayenne Lewis?" I stared at her trying to stash her things into her bag and ignore Palmer. "What happened to her?"

Ari nodded. "I know, right? She looks horrible. That haircut makes her look like a Beijing special-needs orphan. I know she got dropped, that the Fashion Fascists kicked her out of the clique and everything. But come on. Did they go to her house and smash all her mirrors? There's no excuse for looking that militantly tragic."

"Why'd they kick her out?"

Ari shrugged. "Does there have to be a reason?"

I don't know. Didn't there?

I watched her as she rushed toward the exit of the Lecture Hall. Cayenne Lewis, holy shit. I looked closely at her face and could almost recognize it, that profile passing everyone in the hall, never looking at them. Her hair had been really long when she was a Fashion Fascist. She would toss it over her shoulder like she was in a shampoo commercial and laugh. That was probably why I didn't recognize her. That carefree vacant look she had was gone. Now she looked people in the face and dared them to blink.

"I thought she moved away or something," I mumbled.

"Who?" Ari said, then realized I was still talking about Cayenne. "Oh."

Ari let herself get swallowed up in the activity of the Craftsters, and I took a detour to the desk where Cayenne had been sitting. I read what she had written:

Suicide doll's suicide
Pretty, but with death there's no way to hide

Afraid to make a cut, see there's nothing inside
If your friends told you to jump off a bridge
You'd step to the edge and fly.
•–•

I read through it a couple of times. Suicide doll. Even though it was a pretty gruesome poem, I smiled. I glanced at my balloon-face wrist accessory. The dot-dash-dot symbol carved into the plastic desktop looked like the expression on the balloon. Cayenne Lewis had to be connected to the body-drop stunt. Somehow.

My intouch® purred a double-buzz.

mikes: i know how we can catch them. FIND ME. @KID

Mikey was being cryptic, but I knew that strangely we were thinking about the same thing. It happened all the time—it was kind of creepy.

"'Find me,'" I said to myself, opening my notebook® and navigating to Mikey's page. He had a really annoying animation that launched when you clicked.

I glanced at the RIGHT NOW section of his sidebar. He was logged in to the DIY Depot on the fourth floor. And he was a genius.

9 DIY DETECTIVES

Mikey had like a little rat's nest in the DIY Depot, off to the side of the Robot Combat Arena where kids were getting ready for the prizefights tomorrow afternoon. It was the most popular activity in the DIY Depot. Everyone who wanted to compete engineered and built the toughest remote-controlled robots to battle it out in the arena. The current champion robot and its creator were featured at the entrance, along with the hardware supply sponsors who shared in the glory of the tin warrior's continued victory.

I crept carefully into Mikey's nest, eyeballed the wobbly tower of crates filled with electronics parts, and tried to sit where it was least likely to crush me if it fell. Mikey's workspace was hazardous—he left live wires lying around everywhere. The instructors who patrolled the area always reminded him about safety procedures, but Mikey was hard to convince. So they just shook their heads and waited with fire extinguishers ready.

Mikey looked up from soldering something in his little robot's brain.

I peeked over his shoulder at the splayed parts of his combat robot. "He's not going to be ready for the fight tomorrow," I said. It was a statement, but Mikey took it as a question.

"Yeah, of course. Look at him."

Mikey picked up the controllers and made the gimpy robot use two of its working legs to push itself around in a circle on its skateboard wheels.

He laughed maniacally. "It's alive!"

I hit Record, trying to get Mikey's laugh for my collection.

Mikey spent all his time working on the most pathetic little spidery-legged robot. It was raw-clumsy and adorable. Mikey called it Cripple. It got stomped in the arena. We're talking mutilated. Mikey always fixed it up again though.

A Level 16 techboy poked his head over a pile of scrap metal.

"You're wasting your time, Littleton. That spindly little wimp of a robot needs to get scrapped."

"There's nothing wrong with Cripple. *You* need to get scrapped," Mikey muttered while he adjusted the delicate joints in Cripple's skinny knees. "Jerk."

"Hey," I said to Mikey. "Nice deductive skills, Detective Gumshoe." I waved my intouch® in the air, referring to his FIND ME message.

Mikey put his finger to his lips, picked up Cripple's remote control, and moved closer to me.

He spoke quietly, tossing a glance over to the top of the partition making sure that kid didn't pop his head up again.

"I was thinking we could use the log-on tracker in reverse." He fiddled with the knobs on his remote control, testing out all of Cripple's joints and continued in a low voice. "Use the scene of the crime to give us a list of suspects."

"Why are you whispering?" I whispered back.

"Because it could be a conspiracy," he hissed.

I laughed loudly.

"Shh!" he said.

"You don't think it's a conspiracy," I whispered in his ear.

He made a big deal about tucking my hair back behind my ear, then leaned in close. "No," he whispered. "I just think it's really fun to be secretive and pretend to be paranoid."

He leaned back and grinned.

"Yeah, OK." I laughed. But I looked over my shoulder anyway. Maybe it was what that guy said this morning, how "they" were watching us, wanting to know how we made choices. And how my PLAY clue just *happened* to be about the physics of free fall. I was getting good and genuinely paranoid myself.

"But we checked out the scene of the crime yesterday," I said, trying to figure out where we could apply our brilliant new spy technique, "there wasn't anything on the fifth floor besides tampered security cameras."

"Yeah, there was."

Fifth floor, Audio/Viz.

"It's really the only place they could go to edit their film so fast and upload it immediately."

He was right. When I'd linked to the Unidentified video that morning, the time stamp said the film had gone up not even an hour after the event itself. That was a pretty fast turnaround time to edit, render, and upload.

Since notebooks® were only equipped for Network, searching on Archive, and software sponsors' limited-time trial applications, this was the only place that had the resources to pull off the kind of postproduction used for the Unidentified film.

Mikey peeked into the window display at Audio/Viz. There was a single screen showing random clips of films that students had made.

"That's mine. Do you see it?" Mikey said.

I saw a quick close-up of what looked like a cardboard box covered in tinfoil with flashing red lights.

"What's your film about?"

"A zombie movie, except with robots."

I laughed.

We logged in to Audio/Viz. When the light blinked over

83

to green, I was suddenly really aware of how my activity was being tracked inside the Game. Stepping through the doors, I just hoped the same mechanism that let the administrators know where I was right now would give us clues as to who used the equipment yesterday morning.

This room was a lot like the Arcade, except with machines set up with digital video editing software instead of the grabbest online video games.

We walked around the store, not really knowing what we were looking for.

"What are we looking for?"

"I don't know—evidence?" Mikey said, sitting behind a keyboard, pretending to hack.

I laughed. "This is so effing Crime Scene Extreme. Seriously though, is it even *possible* to view log-in records user-side?"

"Hmm, yes," Mikey said tapping his finger on his chin pseudointellectually. "You're right. This sounds like a job for a Crackhead."

Mikey whipped out his intouch® and started writing a message.

mikes: where you playing? @SWIFT

swiftx: arcade @MIKEY

mikes: wanna pop next door, audio/viz? @SWIFT

It was a while before he answered again. I was following the conversation on my intouch®.

swiftx: what is it? i'm about to get promoted @MIKEY

"He's playing Buy, Sell & Destroy," Mikey said, as if I weren't already totally lurking through the entire exchange.

kidzero: please? @SWIFT

I wrote, buttoning in on their conversation again.

swiftx: kid with you? @MIKEY

I was mortified.

mikes: yes. @SWIFT

kidzero: hi. @SWIFT

We looked at each other while we waited for his reply. Mikey mouthed, *You're so rude.*

I knew he was just teasing me, but I felt my face get hot. I usually wasn't that bothered when I made a fool of myself, but this was different. This was Jeremy Swift.

swiftx: let me save my game. @MIKEY, @KID

I smiled at my intouch®. It was such a kick when Jeremy @ed me. I got the same roller-coaster drop in my stomach as I did when he looked at me yesterday.

"Oh, stop," Mikey said, irritated.

"What?"

"'What?'" he mocked.

I punched him on the shoulder, mostly to hide my embarrassment that I apparently wasn't fooling anybody.

Jeremy slouched in through the Audio/Viz doors, hands in his pockets, squinting at everyone from behind his shaggy bangs like the slacker rockstar that he was. He saw Mikey and me and nodded his head in our direction.

We went to meet him.

"What's going on?" Swift said, brushing his hair out of his eyes.

I swallowed. Mikey nudged me.

"Is there any way we could see the Audio/Viz log-in records? We need to see who used the editing stations between like . . . I don't know, the dummy dropped a little after nine," I said.

"Whoa, players don't have access to log-in records," he said. "Why're you asking me?"

"Because you're a Crackhead," Mikey said, emphasizing the "rrr" in Crackhead. "So, come on. Show us the score."

"For yesterday morning. Between, like, nine to eleven a.m.," I added.

"Does this have anything to do with that video you were watching the other day?" Swift said to me.

"Um, yeah," I said, kind of surprised he put it together so quickly. "We're trying to find out who pulled that anti-PR prank yesterday morning. Some group calling themselves the Unidentified."

"Never heard of them," Swift said, shrugging. "Look, log-in records are purged daily after closing time to protect player privacy."

Mikey poked Swift in the chest. "You make a really lousy Crackhead."

Swift slapped Mikey's hand away. "Fawk off."

"So what's our next move?" Mikey asked, turning to me.

I glanced at Jeremy. He was playing around with his intouch®, reading streams. But I caught him peeking over at us. I tried to smile naturally even though I felt like his gaze was pinning my butterfly heart. Seemed like he was interested to know what our next move was too, trying to listen in. Or maybe I was just hoping he was interested.

"I don't know," I admitted.

Jeremy smiled wide. "Hey, have either of you heard anything about an Illegal Arts Workshop today?" he asked.

I shrugged. I didn't know why, but I didn't feel entirely comfortable telling Mikey and Jeremy about my run-in with the mysterious man in the bushes. Okay, the mysterious man and his ex–Fashion Fascist girlfriend. I guess the truth didn't sound as scandalous.

"I've heard rumors," Jeremy said.

"You want to check it out?" Mikey asked me hopefully. "I've got time."

"But we were supposed to meet up with Ari at the Studio."

Mikey rolled his eyes. "How many times this week has Ari blown off band practice? Please express the probability of her being there today in the form of a ratio."

"What, you don't think she's going to come?"

Mikey just shook his head.

I took out my intouch® to let Ari know to meet us in Prime Real Estate instead. I knew she didn't have the greatest track record of making it to practice lately, but I wasn't going to give up on her.

Besides, she'd be upset if we went to an Illegal Arts Workshop without telling her. I passed the word on.

kidzero: change of plans. IAW! tick tock 02, PRE @ARI

"Let's go," I said, feeling kind of guilty that the excitement I felt was more for the idea of hanging out with Swift than learning some forbidden skill.

10 ILLEGAL ARTS WORKSHOP

Illegal Arts Workshops were held in Prime Real Estate, the row of empty storefronts that had been reserved for players to use, to encourage young entrepreneurs to get involved in the joys of retail and business. The kids who got their proposals approved to set up shop in Prime Real Estate sometimes loaned out their space to friends who wanted to share skills that the administrators would never OK. These clandestine activities always got a good turnout. Forbidden knowledge had its allure.

Jeremy walked with us across the hall to the Prime Real Estate wing.

Ari was standing outside one of the storefronts, waiting for us to get there. I waved and her eyes practically ballooned out of her head when she saw us walking with Jeremy.

"Hi, Swift," she said like a sigh.

"Hey," he said quickly, then looked over her head, trying to get a better view at the crowd inside. "See you guys." Swift glanced back over his shoulder at Mikey and me as he slipped inside.

Ari squeezed my arm excitedly and mouthed, *He's so prize.*

"Ready to go in?" I asked, reaching back and grabbing Mikey's hand too.

The swipe card log-in had been disabled, so no record was being kept of who was here. A semifamous newbie with a particular preteen style was holding open the door.

"Hey, I know you," I said, before I could stop myself.

"Do you?" she said icily.

I thought carefully for a minute. She was Lexie Phillips. I knew that, but I guess I didn't really *know* her.

I shrugged. "Right. My mistake."

Lexie took a step back, opening the door wider so the three of us could file in.

There were more kids packed in here than in regularly scheduled, administration-approved workshops. I wondered what we would be learning, and who would be teaching.

We never really got a chance to find out. The lights dimmed a bit and a voice boomed out, distorted through some speakers. "Hey, everyone. Thanks for coming."

Mikey and I exchanged a glance. Illegal Arts Workshops usually weren't so . . . theatrical. Past IAWs involved a

Tinkerer teaching people how to build paint guns or Gear-heads meeting to organize street races. But they all just used the Prime Real Estate classroom as a meeting place, they didn't set up all these smoke and mirrors.

"If everyone could open their notebooks®, we can begin." The teacher voice walked us through the ways to find and use anonymous proxies to get to sites blocked from Archive without a record being kept of our viewing habits. He also helped us install profile trackers to see who visited our pages. Ari looked at me smugly, like she was so far ahead of the illicit trend.

"This will flip the lights on in the dark room on the other side of the two-way mirror. Put the audience in the spotlight." Even though the voice was protectively distorted, the cadence and word choice gave him away. It was the voiceover from the Unidentified video, I was sure of it.

I looked around to see who else was in attendance. As usual, hardly any branded kids showed up. They knew that if their names weren't on the guest list, then it wasn't an event worth going to.

Swift was there, of course. But he was a Crackhead. His sponsors knew he was a "bad boy" when they branded him. It was probably why they did.

Then I saw her. Cayenne Lewis. She was talking to that bore-core girl with the exclamation-point eyebrows who I'd seen in the Pit the day of the dummy drop, and another guy with acne-scarred cheeks wearing a baseball cap.

The voice was talking about how privacy was something

adults didn't think teenagers had a right to, but I couldn't concentrate.

I glanced back across the room to see that Cayenne—

She was looking right at me.

She didn't even look away when I caught her staring, which was the accepted social norm.

So we were locked in an absurd staring contest. I thought of the cameras on the fifth floor, posed in a spy vs. spy stare-down. Then I cracked. I smiled and, strictly following the unwritten rules, lost the staring contest.

Cayenne sort of frowned at me, then turned back to her friends. The girl with the exclamation-point eyebrows had left, and I scanned the crowd to see where she'd gone. I caught a glimpse of her bulky gray sweater heading for the exit, and I had an irrational urge to follow her.

I grabbed my bag and stood up.

"Where are you going?" Mikey asked.

"Um. To the bathroom? Girl stuff," I lied.

Mikey turned back to his screen and looked uncomfortable. "OK, have fun."

"The sponsors put out samples of Time of Your Life® teen tampons at the fourth-floor bathroom," Ari said helpfully. "It's the kind Verity Clark uses."

"Uh, thanks," I said, heading for the door. I wondered how desperate a girl needed to be to allow herself to get branded by a company that makes feminine hygiene products.

11 NETWORK

I pushed my way to the exit and gave Lexie Phillips a lame wave as I passed. I saw the bore-core girl wander toward the escalators, her ankle-length black skirt swishing with each step.

Honestly, I wasn't sure why I was stalking this girl. I just had this feeling. Her being in the Pit during the dummy drop, and hanging out with Cayenne Lewis—a girl I saw practically etching evidence into a desk . . . Something was up, right?

I followed her down to the second floor. She stopped outside of Chez Chess café and banged on the window. I was surprised to see Tycho Williams appear by the exit and swipe his card at the door. Then he rummaged around with something and swiped a second time before stepping out into the hall. He handed the girl one of the cards he had swiped with and they stood and chatted for a while.

Tycho Williams was a legend. It felt stupid, but I was a bit starstruck. He was an amazing street dancer and had his own style that the sponsors snapped up and called "Prep-Hop." Tycho had been wearing thick dark-framed glasses, baggy khaki pants, oversized sneakers, and really tight argyle sweaters long before all the nationwide fashion outlets were selling "the look" off the rack. But I'd heard him doing some mixing in the Studio, and his beats made me a fangirl.

I moved closer to hear what they were saying.

"They almost done?" he asked.

She nodded.

He checked his intouch®. "I need to make an appearance at the VIP Lounge," he said, pointing a loaded finger-gun to his head and pulling the trigger. "Can you watch the door?"

The girl held out her hands and Tycho passed her a bunch of what looked like Game ID cards.

"We'll coordinate later," he said, taking a few strides toward the escalator. She swiped her card and went into Chez Chess café.

I swiped and followed after her. Stepping in, I was hit with the bass rattle of Wu Tang Clan: *"Rraw, I'ma give it t'ya, with no trivia . . ."* They always played classic music in there.

The black-and-white-checked tile floors gleamed. Each

table was filled with two people sitting directly across from each other, staring intensely at the board, sipping coffee. Some tables had a few people hanging around them, watching the games unfold.

The bore-core girl was at the counter explaining to the barista that she wanted her espresso shot, steamed milk, and butterscotch syrup all in separate cups.

The woman behind the counter rolled her eyes and started brewing the beverage.

"You don't think the whole is greater than the sum of its parts?" I asked.

She turned around to look at me. Her eyes were much softer up close, they kind of danced subtly.

"But that doesn't mean you can't appreciate the individual parts for what they are," she said, gathering the three small cups.

"You're friends with Lexie Phillips, right?" I blurted out, hoping to get her to admit how the parts added up.

The guarded look came back. "Lexie has a lot of friends."

"But Cayenne Lewis doesn't have that many. Not anymore. You know her, too, right? And Tycho Williams. You have a lot of popular friends, but I don't know your name."

"It's none of your business," she said, then turned and carried her tiny glasses to a seat by the door.

I smiled. It was like a challenge, and I was determined to find out how Miss None-of-Your-Business fit in with the rest. I found a free table and moved the pieces out from opening position to make room for my notebook®. I logged on to the Network main page.

I started by searching for Lexie Phillips's profile page. And the girl was right, Lexie *did* have a lot of friends. She was ranked in the Top 50 most popular for our school site, which was pretty impressive if she'd only been playing Level 13–17 for a few months. Still, her inflated status was good for me because it meant she had a popularity plug-in that made her page viewable by all. I didn't need to be a "friend" to view her schedule or content. People in the Top 50 were so popular that privacy was a status no longer available to them. I scrolled through Lexie's list of friends, but there were so many. There was no way I was going to find bore-core girl's name on that list.

I scanned through the other parts of Lexie's profile. She kept a weird page. None of the interests she listed made sense. She said she was into the history of plumbing through the ages, tracking weather patterns, and practicing echolocation. Under her Content Accomplishments she said she was proud of her ability to bench-press 208 pounds. Her Hopes and Dreams included one day discovering a species of tiny frog that had moth wings, and trampolining on cumulous clouds.

I lol'd. She had filled her entire profile page with an overload of nonsense information, never once mentioning her Save the Princess team score, or who her best friend was, or anything real. I wondered if she felt the same way about those things as I did about my music, or if she just liked effing with people. Still, I had to admit, I kind of secretly wished she actually was a sonar-navigating, cloud-bouncing meteorologist with antlike strength.

I looked at her sidebar.

"I knew it," I said to myself.

Her RIGHT NOW status said she was here in Chez Chess café. I texted Mikey.

kidzero: a breakthrough. is IAW done? @MIKEY

mikes: almost. you ok? @KID

kidzero: yeah. can you see lexie phillips? @MIKEY

mikes: who? @KID

kidzero: nvm. @MIKEY

I did a profile search for Cayenne Lewis while I waited to see who would show up to claim their IDs. I would probably only get to see her limited public profile, but you never knew. She had been branded once, so she might have a popularity plug-in too.

Cayenne's page was private, but if the profile statistics were accurate, then no one could see her page.

It said she had zero friend connections.

That didn't make sense. I was a nobody, and even I had a few friends. Besides, I'd seen her hanging out with people . . . people's identities I'd hoped to find out through her friend list, actually.

I stared at the round, empty zero by her name, and the message *Cayenne Lewis has no friends.*

But I didn't feel sorry for her. I knew that couldn't be true. I just . . . I didn't understand why she wouldn't admit that she had friends.

My friends list on my Network page was pretty pathetic. The only friend connections I really cared about were Ari and Mikey, and Jeremy. Oh, and Tesla's updates were always really entertaining, even though I didn't consider her a supertight friend.

The other maybe five or six links were people I didn't even really know. They were just some random kids in the Game who at one point popped up on my user page with the message "so-and-so wants to be your friend" and I clicked the *"uh . . . ok."* option just to be nice. We weren't exactly having sleepovers or anything.

But I could click to their pages if I wanted, subscribe to their streams and read their daily entries, see where they were currently logged in, and view their private profiles. I clicked Ari's out of habit.

I read yesterday's post, the one she was sure a cool hunter was interested in. It was about kickboxing and her flirty-and-tough look. She went into a lot of detail about her pink training gloves that she embroidered with Hello Kitty faces with bruises and black eyes, and how she came up with the "kick-ass ballerina" look by wrapping her bare legs with satin ribbons. She posted a lot of photos of herself play-kicking the camera and winking. She really knew how to play the game.

There was a knock on the Chez Chess café window and I saw the bore-core girl try to shoo away the boy with the baseball cap waiting for her outside. She glanced over to my table and I wiggled my fingers in an innocent wave.

I clicked back to the Network main page with the ranking of everyone in the school. Palmer Phillips, Eva Bloom, and Abercrombie Fletcher were at the top of the list, as always. The ranking only takes into account how many friends someone reports having.

Then I had an idea.

I scrolled all the way to the bottom of the status list, looking for Cayenne's name.

And there it was. But she wasn't the only one in our Level 13–17 site who reported having zero friends. There were two other names on the bottom of the list. I could have been way wrong about this, but I suspected that I was looking at the names of the Unidentified.

I studied the names on my notebook® screen:

Elijah Carmichael

Sophia Carvalho

Cayenne Lewis

People friend one another all the time just to make it look like they rank. A person needed to make an active effort to have zero friends.

I copied the names and added Lexie and Tycho to the list. Lexie Phillips wasn't on the zero-friends list, but she

had a Chez Chess alibi. Tycho Williams, too. That was probably Elijah at the window, and Sophia sulking across the
room.

But I was still missing *him*. The Illegal Arts instructor,
the voice of the Unidentified. Who was he?

I felt someone standing behind me, looking over my
shoulder. I closed my notebook® and turned around.
Jeremy Swift was standing there, holding two cups of
coffee.

"Hey," I said.

"Hey." He held up a cup. "I was just getting an espresso
injection and I saw you. You want?"

"Oh, yeah. Thanks."

I took a sip. It was hot and milky, and perfectly sweet,
just how I liked it.

"I read how you took your coffee on your profile," he
admitted. I nearly choked on the warm beverage. Jeremy
Swift had been checking out *my* profile page? I didn't know
whether to be flattered or embarrassed.

"What did you think of the IAW?" I coughed out, trying
to change the subject.

He smiled cryptically. "Oh. I thought it was very infor-
mative."

I laughed nervously to fill the awkward silence. "So,
um," I began. "Were you just lurking or . . . ?"

"I wasn't lurking," he began, kind of defensively. Then
full of his high-score confidence again, continued, "Actually, I wanted to ask you . . . Elle told me you had a cache of

hours saved up. Any chance I could trade with you? Credit or something?"

I felt kind of stupid. Jeremy didn't search my profile because he was interested in me; he was interested in how many online hours I had.

"So," he said when I didn't answer. "Is there anything I can help you with?" He leaned in close. "Favors for favors?"

"Yeah, maybe," I squeaked out, a parade of make-out session images flashed in my mind. I shook them away.

"What're you working on?" he asked, blowing on his coffee.

"Nothing. I was just waiting for someone." I glanced at the table by the door, but saw that she was gone. Sophia. I blew it. She probably knew I was up to something with all my questions.

"You still looking for the people who made that film?"

I nodded cautiously.

"Why?" he said. The trickiest of all questions.

"I don't know." I shrugged. "Don't you think it's interesting?"

"Dangerous, more like."

Dangerous for who? I wanted to ask. But I played with my intouch® instead, while I tried to decide how much I wanted to involve Swift in my search.

toy321: re: flipstream. crybaby pharme-sponsors urged admin for the ban.

#spons: blink-of-an-eye tech testing stations installed in the arcade. focus your brain for score!

mikes: studio time? @KID

"I should go. I've got Studio time reserved."

"Wait." He grabbed my wrist, but let go quickly. I could still feel the warm, dry sensation where he touched me. I almost wanted to look to see if it made a mark. "What are you doing tomorrow? You want to do something?"

Swift wanted to "do something" with me?

"Maybe we can make a trade?" he said. "A little time for a little time?"

He meant my online hours again.

"Sure," I said getting up. "Thanks for the coffee."

He started saying, "Yeah, and about that . . ."

Then: "I mean, no problem."

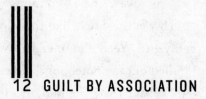

12 GUILT BY ASSOCIATION

"Where's Ari?" I asked Mikey when I got to the Studio.

"Guess," he said.

I checked my intouch® and saw that Ari's last update was from the Sweatshop.

> **aria:** added evil studs and grommets to ballet slippers. now i can grand jeté yr ass.

I called her out.

> **kidzero:** we're waiting for you in the studio. you're coming, yeah? please please @ARI

Mikey sat behind the drum kit tossing his drumstick and dropping it. Repeatedly.

"She won't come," he said.

"She will."

Toss. Drop.

"You okay?" he asked me.

I wasn't. I didn't like this cloudy feeling of uncertainty in my gut. "Yeah, I'm fine," I answered. "Look what I found." I pulled out my notebook® and showed him the list.

"What's that?" he said, moving closer to read the words on my screen.

"Names of the people who were involved in the dummy drop stunt. I think."

Mikey read through the names.

"Tycho Williams? Yeah, right," he said skeptically. "How did you find these?"

I tried to explain the connections, the coincidences, and the clues that I used to compile the list. When I said it aloud to Mikey it didn't sound as convincing as in my head.

"Who else did you show this to?" he asked.

"No one. Why?"

Mikey shrugged. "What if people thought I was a point-grubbing, hyperambitious brand-gawker just because I was in a band with Ari?"

I got angry. "What's your problem? Ari's, like, my best friend. Why are you down on her all the time?"

Mikey held up his hands defensively. "I'm just saying, guilt by association is not a game. Accusing people of stuff without evidence, just based on who they were seen hanging out with? What if the administrators end their game and it's not them?"

"You think they'd get Game Over for a stunt like that?"

"Just . . . I'd hate for my name to show up on a suspect list without a chance to explain myself, you know?"

Mikey was zapping all the fun out of my spy game. Maybe I should've asked Swift to play instead; he seemed to at least think it was exciting.

"Hey, how long have you known Swift?" I asked, trying to remember how much I'd confided in him about my Unidentified search.

"Why? Do you like him?" Mikey teased.

"No, I just—I don't know."

"He's a jerk."

"What? He's your friend. Why are you friends with him if you think he's a jerk?"

"All my friends are jerks. It doesn't mean you should date any of them."

"I'm not going to date Swift," I said, embarrassed now. "Besides, what do you care? What makes you think I'm even interested—"

"Boring," Mikey said, interrupting me the way he usually did when he didn't want to continue a conversation.

The light on the door flashed green and Ari sulked in. I was weirdly relieved to see her.

"Yay! We're all here," I said, getting up to give her a hug. "Listen to this." I played the bird-wing drum track from the other day. "It definitely needs your analog touch. Something woodwindy?"

Ari listened, a little distractedly.

"It's too weird," she said.

"What?"

"The beat is too weird. It's too random. Have you heard this?" She played an *Idol* band's latest track with a relentless and deeply monotonous rhythm. "It should be more like that, right?"

"I don't know," I said. "It sounds a little too Pathe-techno . . ."

"That's what people want to listen to. Something—"

"We're not an *Idol* band, Aria." Mikey said her name like the opera solo, the way her parents intended.

"*Ar-ee-ah,*" she corrected. Pronouncing it like Maria but without the *M*. "And no kidding we're not an *Idol* band. You guys keep changing our band name so no one's even heard of us." She pressed Play and the *Background Checks* track I was going to ask them to help me with started up. "We're never going to get any airplay with this kind of weird sound stuff."

"But what's the fun in sounding like everything else?" I asked her. "Or just sounding the way people expect us to sound?"

She just sighed dramatically.

"You gonna start breaking glass, diva-style?" Mikey screeched out a note.

I covered my ears. "Mikey, stop!"

Mikey shut up. Then he put down his drumsticks and got up to leave.

"Wait," I said, frustrated that he was taking off when we were finally all together.

"I'll be in the DIY Depot," he mumbled, before leaving.

Ari mouthed the word *Diva* and checked her intouch®.

I was so disappointed that we didn't get anything done. I loved both Mikey and Ari, loved who they were and what they could do musically, but it was so frustrating that we couldn't work together to make something amazing. I mean, I could already *hear* what the music of all of us together would sound like. I just needed them to play it.

"Hey," Ari said, "the Craftsters are going shopping. You don't want to come, right?"

Behind Ari, I saw Mr. Levy walking down the corridor with a man who had the calculated casual look of a cool hunter. Was that the Hit List cool hunter, Murdoch West? I didn't want to talk to them, and definitely didn't want to have the conversation with Ari in the room.

"Yeah, yeah. Let's go!" I said, gathering up my stuff at record speed.

"Really? You never—" she said, moving too slowly.

"Come on," I said, holding open the door for her. Mr. Levy caught sight of me and waved me over. I waved back like I didn't know what he meant, and hurried Ari out of the Studio.

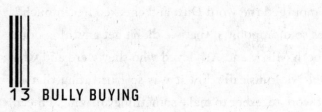

13 BULLY BUYING

Ari, Avery, Kasi, Tesla, and I all piled into Tesla's car. Rocket decided to hang out with Palmer and some of the other kids from Generation Triple-A instead. I could tell Ari was in a bad mood because she was being louder than usual. More forcibly joyful. She flipped through the music stations, demanding something unrelentingly upbeat.

"What're you doing?" Ari asked me.

"Turning off my intouch®. My mom's been checking up on my GPS all the time lately."

"Here. Gimme," Tesla said, holding her hand out, but keeping her eyes on the road. "Force-quitting your intouch® is a newbie trick." She synched my intouch® with her car's GPS. "Elle finally launched the Alibi app she's been working on. Where do you live?"

I recited my home coordinates, and Tesla programmed in a route to my house on her dash.

"You can also use the mapping software on Archive to set coordinates," she said, passing it back to me. "There you go. Evidence that would hold up in a court of law."

"Cheater," Ari said, grinning. She pounded on the back of the driver's seat. "Thanks for driving the getaway car, Tess."

"Yeah. Thanks, Tesla," I said softly. I held tight to my intouch®, feeling strangely weightless. Invisible.

Free.

I thought about the Unidentified list and felt like I understood their misleading card-swiping better. It wasn't fair of me to suspect them of trouble just because they didn't want administrators keeping track of their every move. Sometimes a little deception was necessary to get out of being watched all the time.

"How did you hack the ignition?" Ari asked Tesla. "My parents put a lock on my car so I can't drive out of the Game before four."

"Oh, my parents didn't set driver controls," she explained.

"Really? And no one called Child Protective Services?" Ari joked. "I wish my parents trusted me. It's not like I'm going to quit out of the Game early and drive off."

"Um. We kind of *are* quitting out of the Game early and driving off." Kasi laughed from the front seat.

"Wooo!" Avery called out the window.

I liked being squeezed together with these girls. Speeding down a highway with the music up and windows down. I wished it always felt like that, like a FreshFlash® commercial for pinky-sized digital cameras with extra-memory for raw image enhancement to keep the colors bright and smiles genuine.

We drove into the city, Tesla completely keeping her cool in the insanely merging and stopping traffic thanks to all the hours she logged on the Urban Driving simulator in the Game. When we got close to the Boulevard, Tesla pressed the button on a parking locator she had been developing with some Modgeeks and Gearheads in the DIY Depot. Since the new parking meters allowed mobile payment options, she had been working to isolate the frequency given off by a receptive meter to indicate non-occupied spots.

A few blinking dots appeared on her GPS mapping screen showing her the location of free spaces.

We spilled out of the car and gaggled toward the shops. Ari grabbed my hand and pulled me along.

"Let's go. Hurry. I want to get to Trendsetters. I saw some shoes there that are *mine*."

I smiled. A determined Ari was a happy Ari.

I didn't come downtown very often. There wasn't anything to do. Practically all the shops had NO ONE UNDER 17 ALLOWED signs illuminated in their storefronts. Everyone said it was for our own protection, that they couldn't guarantee the content of the stores were safe for underage consumers, so it was best if we were locked out. But I had seen how shopkeepers watched us when we passed. Like we were criminals for just being there.

Kasi was demonstrating a combo move for a two-person fighter game while we walked down the street, against the salmon flows of adult commuters. They frowned at us as we moved forward, laughing.

"But you should see how Lexie does it," Tesla said. "She's one of the skillest players I've ever played with."

"What's she like?" I asked, thinking maybe her teammates could help me sort out the truthful inaccuracies of her Network profile.

"I don't know. Quiet?" Tesla said, focused on her intouch®. "She's got scary dead-on aim."

"I think it's because she's filled with rage," Kasi joked.

"What?"

"Just don't bother trying to be friends with her," Kasi said. "I mean, everyone always tries to buddy up with her to get close to Palmer. It won't work."

"I wasn't going to. I—"

"Oh come on, Kid. You're a fame whore like the rest of us. Don't play." Ari let go of my hand and demonstrated an alternative kick-punch combo and managed to direct-hit a lady's oversized gray leather handbag.

"Sorry!" she squealed after her, then muttered, "I wouldn't have hit your bag if it wasn't so ugly and elephantine."

In the Trendsetters store, we all flashed our Game

IDs to the shop assistant and the lady's suspicious frown morphed into a servile smile. Trendsetters clothing had been a Game sponsor since the beginning. Thanks to the partnership, we were welcome here.

"What are you girls shopping for today?"

"Shoes," Kasi said decisively.

"A jacket," Tesla said, already checking the racks.

"Skinny jeans," Avery answered.

"Whatever!" Ari gushed.

They all turned to look at me. I wasn't really planning on buying anything, I just came for the social activity of it all.

"We'll help her," Ari said knowingly.

The lady went over to the jeans section with Avery since she was going to be requiring the most assistance getting her thighs into skinny jeans.

I flipped through things on the rack. I liked the colors, liked looking at the styles, but I couldn't imagine myself in any of them. Especially when I scanned the barcode with my intouch® plug-in. I couldn't afford anything in here.

The Craftsters were going to mod their purchases once they got back into the Game, put their individual handmade touches on their new clothes, but the whole place reeked of Fashion Fascist. Sometimes I really didn't get the clique wars.

Ari bounded up beside me, hangers clothed in sweaters and dresses gripped in each hand.

"Did you find anything?" I asked.

"Yep. These are for you," she shoved one collection of

hangers into my arms. "Come on. Let's go try them on."

We shared a large dressing room and pulled off our clothes. I turned around and saw Ari was wearing matching yellow satin bra and panties. On the ass of the underwear there was a silk-screened handprint. It looked like a greasy man-hand had grabbed her butt.

"Are those new?" I asked.

She turned around to view her ass in the mirror. "Yeah, aren't they dirty?"

I nodded, not really knowing how to answer. I looked through the clothes Ari had chosen for me. The legs of the pants she got me were nearly twice as long as my own now-seemingly-stubby legs. And none of the shirts seemed quite up to the challenge of covering up enough skin to qualify as a garment.

I pulled the eggplant-and-lime-colored too-tight shirt off over my head.

"What do you think of this?"

Ari was wearing a button-up-the-front dress with a dramatic collar. The collar looked kind of good with her short-styled hair, but the overall impression was of an evil galactic overlord.

"It's definitely a look," I said, not daring to offer an opinion.

I pulled an army green tank dress on over my head and turned to look in the mirror. It really was cute. There was a tangerine racing stripe down the side. And the skirt had a flirty little flip to it. I kind of liked it.

"Oh! You should get that! Kid, you look adorable."

"Yeah, it's pretty grab, but when would I ever wear it?"

"All. The. Time," she said enthusiastically.

I scanned the barcode to check the price.

"Ari, I can't afford this."

"What do you mean? You can just put it on your Game card."

Our Game IDs doubled as credit cards inside and out-side of the Game, something my mom discovered after the bill came during my first year in the Game. All the swipes to get tokens for the Vending Machine snacks and drinks at the cafés and Culture Shock meals really added up.

"Why can't you put it on your Game card?" Ari said, zipping up some Dance Riot–inspired pants. The whole right hip area was shredded and discolored like she had been dragged across the floor.

I didn't really want to explain it to Ari. Her parents were happy to pay the bills on whatever she wanted. She didn't have to explain to them how important it was to have the right things in a place like the Game—they already knew the price of success.

"My mom would be pissed," I said, looking in the mirror again.

"Put it on your Game card," she said, like a command.

I laughed and turned to face her.

"Buy it," she said seriously.

I rolled my eyes and started to take it off. Ari stepped forward, close, entering my space. "Come on, you have to get it," she said, her face close to mine. Her face melted into her charming smile. "It looks so prize on you," she said sweetly. And stepped back into her corner to finish trying on her things.

I felt a little sick handing over my Game card to the lady, and refused to even look at the printout of how much I'd just charged. Thanks to added peer-pressure purchasing, I walked out of there with silver-and-black-striped leggings and red slip-on flats to go with the dress. When Tesla dropped me off, I ran in to hide the shopping bag in my room before Mom got home.

"Kid!" I heard her call through my bedroom door a few minutes later.

"Yeah?"

"Did you feed Lump?"

"Yeah," I said, even though I hadn't. I felt bad about lying to my mom, but I didn't want her to know I'd gone downtown. I felt worse about the hungry dog in the other room and vowed to slip him his food when my mom left the room.

"Look what I got you," she said, opening my door. "I saw a show the other night that said how popular these are right now. On sale!"

I cringed, waiting to see what it was. She held up a pink plaid sundress that Eva Bloom would wear if that look hadn't gone out of style seven weeks ago.

"Isn't it cute? I'm going to have to take a few more shifts at Aunt Gillie's to pay it off, but I want you to have the best."

"Yeah. Thanks, Mom," I mumbled. I wanted to feel grateful, I knew she tried. But she should realize I was not going to get any popularity points from something she got on discount. "I just need to finish up some schoolwork."

"OK, Kiddie. Play hard." She kissed the top of my head, then left my room, closing the door behind her.

I scanned the tag with my intouch®. The pink thing cost a pathetic fraction of what I'd just spent at Trendsetters.

I opened my notebook® to check Trendsetters' return policies, but I got distracted by the little spying eyeball icon in the corner of my Network page. It was the tracker app I had installed in the Illegal Arts Workshop earlier today. I clicked it and scrolled through to see who had been viewing my page.

My privacy settings were friends-only, so I wasn't surprised to see Mikey and Ari topping the list. My heart started bumping hummingbird style when I saw that Swift had checked me out a few times in the past couple days. I couldn't wait to tell Ari.

I scrolled through to Recent Views and was surprised to see that apparently sponsors were an exception to the friends-only privacy setting. Protecht Securities and Trendsetter clothing had recently viewed my page. The Trendsetter sponsors probably had a policy to look at a page after a Game purchase was made in their stores. But why would Protecht Securities be interested in my content?

Then, as I was logged on and watching, a new address

popped up into the viewing field. *Zeronet*. I'd never heard of them, but they must've had sponsor status because they definitely weren't on my friends list.

As the eyeball icon pulsed slowly, I got a little spooked that someone I didn't know was looking at my page at the same time as I was. It almost made me feel like they could see into my bedroom, right now.

My notebook® pinged as a new private message appeared in my inbox.

They've got their eyes on you now. And so do I.
by anonymous

The words jolted me deep like a static shock. I logged out quickly and closed my notebook®. I was too creeped out to know how to reply. I didn't think it was even possible to create an anonymous account on Network.

Then I remembered the Illegal Arts Workshop.

Obviously there were ways to get around the Network security systems. Anonymous proxies to hide the identities of the viewer. But I'd seen who had been looking at my page.

Zeronet.

14 TRENDSPOTTER

"Why aren't you wearing your new clothes?" Ari asked when I met her for breakfast in Culture Shock the next day. Our mornings there were kind of a tradition. Or they had been, until she got cliqued.

"I don't know," I said, taking a seat beside her. "It felt a little too dressy for school."

"It wasn't. It was totally the look you need right now to get noticed."

I had been thinking about that anonymous private message all night, and I was pretty confident that I would prefer not to be noticed, thank you very much.

"Did you get me my cream cheese steamed bun?" I asked.

"No. I was there with you in that dressing room, and what kind of friend would I be if I fed you fat-filled steamed buns?"

"An *amazing* friend?" I pleaded. "I'm craving one so bad right now."

She just shook her head. "Eat this. Much more healthy." She pushed a plate with a green-tinged pastry over to me.

The World Languages Department required students to order foreign food in the native language. It was supposed to provide us with the "experience of travel," which apparently meant being really confused and reduced to universal hand-gestures to express what you needed. Lucky for the Culture Shock program, the food was reeeally good, like worth-making-a-fool-of-yourself good. If you couldn't learn the language, the alternative was making friends with someone who could order, that was another one of the "rainbow diversity" goals of the World Languages Department.

I could squeak out enough Italian to order gelato, but Ari learned Japanese so she could order sushi and video chat with an e-pal in Kyoto so she should be like the poster child of the Culture Shock program. Mikey knew a brand of East LA Spanish slang he picked up from watching too many Hollywood gang flicks. They were pretty much my only friends, so I survived on sushi, pizza, burritos, and hamburgers. I wondered if it was also the aim of the World Languages Department that the socially maladjusted go hungry.

I bit into the Japanese pastry Ari ordered for me. It was good but it wasn't amazing.

All Ari wanted to do during our "together time" was talk about strategies on how to get branded. I scrolled through my intouch® messages, but there were only some sponsor messages and a call-to-arms from Tesla. She'd found out who lobbied for the ban on her product.

toy321: re: flipstream. message swarm PEDIAFIX. tell them goggles are for recreational use only. go! go! go!

I thumbed in a protest message to PediaFix®, and half-listened to Ari tell me about what Rocket had told her about the VIP Lounge.

"She makes it sound like the whole place is coated with pixie dust," I said, sipping my tea.

"Yes, pixie dust and power." She sighed dreamily. I couldn't tell if she was joking. "I wish my tracker was still working," she said, flicking her notebook® screen as if that would help. "I don't know if Aerwear has been back to my page. I posted images of my punk ballet slippers and everything—"

"Your tracker's not working?"

"Yeah, I think admin found out about it and blocked it."

I opened my notebook® to check, even though I swore to myself that I wouldn't. The eyeball icon was gone.

"It worked last night," I said more to myself than to Ari. "Do you think someone who was at the IAW yesterday told?"

"Who would tell?" Ari said, tearing off a piece of her

pastry and popping it in her mouth.

Yeah. I didn't know. I thought about the Illegal Arts Workshop, about the voice telling us how to subvert Network security.

"Have you ever heard of Zeronet?" I asked Ari.

"Nuh-uh," she said, shaking her head and trying to lick powdered sugar off her lips and fingertips.

"They visited my page last night."

"Huh," she said, obviously not interested.

"You know who else visited my page?" I dangled the scrap of gossip out to get her attention. "Jeremy Swift."

"No way," she said, frowning. "Let me see."

"I can't. The tracker's down."

Then her tone got sharp. "Well, that's convenient."

"What's that supposed to mean?"

Ari laughed a fake and tinkly kind of laugh. "Seriously, Kid. If you want to start rumors about Jeremy being interested in you, there has to be at least *some* possibility of it being true."

I looked at Ari. Looked at her glittery violet eyes, so different from the hazel ones I had looked into when we used to tell each other secrets and confessed our crushes. They weren't the same eyes that cried for me when I was having problems at home. Not the same eyes that winked at me when we were pulling pranks on Mikey.

"I'm just trying to look out for you," she said.

"Right," I said quietly.

My intouch® hummed in my hand.

"Anyway, I have to go." I picked up my bag, getting ready to leave.

"What? Where are you going? We never get to hang out anymore," she complained. I looked at her to see if she was serious. *She* was the one who kept blowing off band practice with me and Mikey to hang out with Rocket and the Craftsters.

"Winterson wants to see me." I quickly slammed back the last of my tea.

She looked irritated. "Fine, then. Next time you can order your own *matcha manju*."

My eyes were watering. The tea had been way too hot.

I headed over to Winterson's office, humiliated. I was pissed at Ari, mostly because she was probably right. Who was I trying to fool? Swift was just interested in my excess online hours, it was stupid to think it was anything else.

I slumped down in the chair across from Winterson and waited for the "big announcement."

She stared at me quietly for a moment. "Katey," she began, "earlier this week you asked me about suicide. . . ."

"I'm not depressed, if that's what you think," I said quickly.

"No, no. After our talk I asked around a little in headquarters to see what was going on. The sponsors weren't

122

responsible for that stunt last week, in case you were still wondering."

Nope. I wasn't still wondering. That was stale news.

"But because of our conversation," Winterson said, biting her pinky nail, "the sponsors got interested and began their own investigation to find more information."

"No one was interested," I said. "No one cared."

"Well, that's actually what I'm trying to tell you. *You* were interested in it." Winterson rubbed her temples. "Let me back up. I just wanted you to know that it wasn't my intention to bring more attention to this suicide phenomenon . . . or you."

I wished she would get to the point already.

"They want to brand you, Katey."

"What?"

"It's in your record now that you are a trendspotter. The sponsors will be keeping a closer eye on you from now on."

"What? I was just logged in to my record. I didn't see anything in my record about being a trendspotter."

"It won't be made public user-side until you accept their terms and conditions. But it's in there, Katey."

I didn't like the idea of information about me being in my record that I couldn't see or edit. And I didn't have anything to do with that suicide stunt. I was just an innocent bystander or something.

"But there were tons of kids in the Pit who saw it happen, how could I get credit for 'spotting' it?"

Winterson sighed heavily. "You were the first one to

talk about it. To show interest. To search for it. The flow of interest is what the sponsors follow. They already had your notebook® registered as the first video view."

I thought about the anonymous private message: *They've got their eyes on you now.*

"We've contacted your mom," Winterson began. "You'll be meeting with the administrators and interested sponsors' brand representatives today after closing time."

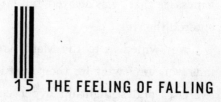

15 THE FEELING OF FALLING

"Kid?"

I turned to see Jeremy waiting outside Winterson's office.

"Hey, what are you doing here?"

"What are you doing right now?" he said.

"I don't know." I was supposed to meet Mikey in the DIY Depot. He was going to battle in the Robot Combat Arena today.

"Oh. I thought maybe you'd want to do that thing we talked about yesterday. In Chez Chess."

I didn't know what he meant.

"Favors for favors?" he said smiling. "I thought we could do an hours trade. I saw that you've been stuck in Math

Attack. You want to play?"

I'll admit I was flattered that Swift wanted to spend time with me, but I wished he'd chosen a mission a little more romantic than math.

"Yeah, OK," I said pulling out my intouch®. I left Mikey a message that I was delayed, but I'd be there before Cripple entered the ring.

We swiped in to the Math Attack prep room, where kids were reviewing for their next level—doing meditation exercises and straight-up hyperventilating. I took a deep breath and walked with him to a free table.

"I got some Study Aides® off of Archive. Can I see your notebook®?"

Yes, the date had gotten off to a truly romantic start. Ari was so right. I took a seat beside him and slid my notebook® over to him.

I peeked nervously into the Math Attack area while he installed the Study Aides®. It was a bit like the Arcade up on fifth—where the SimKids plan cities, raise families and destroy military targets—but down here there was a lot more anxiety. Kids stared into video monitors, typing in their calculations, cringing when they pressed Send, like a bomb was about to go off.

The install finished and Jeremy looked away from the screen and at me.

"Do you want something?" He said, leaning in closer.

I kind of wanted his lips on my neck, but I didn't tell him that. Instead I said, "What?"

He nodded toward the wall display of Liquid Crack® and Focus® drug samples.

"No, thanks. I'm OK."

He looked disappointed. "Well, would you mind if I swiped with your card? They're free," he said quickly, seeing the hesitation on my face. "I just maxed out my sample allotment on my card, that's all."

"Oh. Sure," I said, sliding my card over to him.

He went to the display and got a two-pill sample packet. "You sure you don't want?"

I shook my head.

He shrugged and took both of them. I watched his neck as he swallowed them dry.

He smiled at me. "Ready to do this?"

Jeremy positioned my notebook® in between us and I watched his lips move as he pointed to equations, trying to help me work out a strategy to defeat the end stage and pass the level. He hunched over the screen, frowning and intense.

He looked up at me. "You getting all of this?"

"I guess."

"Come on. Think of it like a puzzle, or code. You just need to figure out the right pieces to make it work."

He moved his chair closer to mine, leaned in close with the Study Aide®. Even though this didn't exactly help me concentrate on math, my senses focused to take in the whole experience of being near him. A kind of contact high, or something. I could feel his arm resting on the back of my chair. His shirt smelled like cotton and cinnamon, and something else. Like welded metal or outer space. With him sitting beside me, I was hyperaware of everything. And when I stared at the problems in front of us, I could understand what he was showing me.

I found the puzzle piece that fit.

"You ready?"

I nodded and swiped my ID at the VR grapher, the redesigned flight simulator that ran the Functions Graphing program I needed to pass to get to the next level. I climbed into the cockpit and strapped in, the harness tight across my shoulders. I looked at the dark screen, gripped the controls in my sweaty hands, and breathed out. It felt like I had been holding my breath for the past forty minutes.

I waited for Jeremy to shut the door so the program would start. He ran his hand nervously through his hair, looked around quickly, then jumped into the capsule, pulling the door shut behind him.

"What are you doing!?"

"Coming along for the ride." He laughed. His laugh sounded like rain clouds clearing.

The countdown had begun. *10 . . . 9 . . .*

"But you don't have a belt!"

"Come on, you can't expect me to spend the morning studying Quadratic Functions, and not get to ride?" he said, trying to maneuver in the cramped capsule.

His knee jabbed into my thigh.

"Oops, sorry," he said.

6 . . . 5 . . . 4 . . .

I started laughing, a little maniacally. This wasn't how I imagined playing the final stage.

"You can do this, easy," he said, bracing his arm against the ceiling and looking at the screen.

"Here we go!" I practically shouted as the capsule started vibrating.

3 . . . 2 . . . 1 . . .

The first equation appeared on the screen and the timer started counting down. I had to do fifteen equations in twenty minutes.

I did the work, finding the vertex and plugging in various values of x to find y. I plotted the coordinates. Hit Submit.

The capsule tilted back and, together with the screen graphic, gave the illusion of acceleration along a gently curving parabola, first down, then back up.

"Whee," he said flatly.

I graphed two more functions, and we rode their paths like a carnival ride. The adrenaline of the time pressure and Jeremy close beside me added to the thrill that I was getting them right.

Then I saw the fourth function.

"Oh Google," I swore. "Look at the leading coefficient! It's negative!" I glanced quickly at Jeremy. He swallowed, his Adam's apple bobbing.

"It'll be way steep, too," he said, staring at the screen, calculating it in his head. Then he looked around the capsule trying to position himself better. "Just solve it like the other ones."

"OK," I said, plotting the coordinates. "Ready?"

The parabola was opened upside down and we were about to climb and then plunge down the side of it. I hesitated before hitting Submit.

"Do it!" he said.

The whole capsule tilted violently backward as we moved up the path. Jeremy slid up out of the seat and bumped his head on the ceiling. When we got to the vertex and plunged over the edge, my breath caught in my throat. It felt like we were falling face-first off the side of a cliff.

Then we leveled out for the next function.

"Good game," Jeremy said, rubbing the back of his head. His dark, messy hair was getting even messier. "Hurry! Watch your time!"

I went on to the next function, then the next. I knew what I had to do now and could actually get them done pretty fast. Probably because every time I hit Submit and the animation-ride sequence started up, Jeremy took my hand from the controllers and we yelled our lungs out as we plunged down each function's course. I would do anything for more moments like those, even math endgames.

When the last function had been graphed, the capsule settled to a halt. My scores scrolled by on the screen. I got only one wrong, and that was Jeremy's fault because he had been shifting around and hit the Submit button before I was ready. My time bonus was surprisingly high too.

At last, the words every girl wants to see after rocketing around in a capsule with a cute boy: LEVEL COMPLETE.

Jeremy moved closer, if that was possible, and said quietly to me. "Good game. Now, um, if you don't mind opening the door, I'd like to unfold myself."

I unstrapped my safety belt and opened the door, peeking around Math Attack to make sure there weren't any supervisors roaming around. We didn't want my level score to be invalidated because there were too many pilots in the cockpit. Someone might've thought we were cheating.

"That was click," Jeremy said, stretching. "So fun."

It wasn't impossible to cheat in the Game. Theoretically, you could just hand your ID to a particularly smart and morally ambiguous friend and watch your points add up. But if you did that you'd miss out on this *feeling* of passing a level. It was an endorphin rush I wouldn't want to trade away. After hours or days or weeks of frustration and perseverance and insanity, somehow doing it. Getting another step closer to beating the Game.

I checked my intouch®. I'd missed a lot of updates from Mikey while I was rocketing around with Swift.

mikes: is polishing the world's next robotic prize-fighting champ!

mikes: is sending our hero into the ring!

Oh no. I was missing the beginning of the battle.

"Good game," Jeremy said when we had logged out of Math Attack.

"You said that already," I said, still glowing with my accomplishment.

"I meant about getting branded."

I sobered up quick. "That hasn't been made public yet."

He laughed. "Oh, right." He took my hand in his. "It's just that Protecht Securities is my sponsor too, so I kind of knew they were interested in you."

I was quiet, thinking about it. So Protecht Securities wanted to brand me?

"I thought it made sense," he said, shrugging. "If we were both branded by the same company. You know, *together?*"

He squeezed my hand a little bit. In my other hand, Mikey was demanding my attention.

mikes: is suffering a devastating loss.

mikes: why aren't you here? @KID

16 LAST LAUGH

Mikey was at his workspace in DIY Depot. He was kind of just staring off into space when I walked in.

"Oh no! Is that Cripple?" There was a box of mangled metal parts on Mikey's work table.

"Yeah," Mikey said, bowing his head in respect. "He fought a good fight. Where were you?"

"Sorry I missed it," I said, evading the question. I glanced at the beloved's mechanical remains, now barely recognizable as scrap metal. "What're you going to do now?"

"Fix him up again. The little guy is powered by pure fight."

That wasn't technically true, Cripple had battery packs, but Mikey was definitely driven by something I didn't fully understand. "Mikey. Hey, Mikey?" I said.

He looked up from his circuit board.

"Way to be my best friend."

He grinned. "Aww . . . high five!"

We reached up to five each other, but missed. I knocked over a small box filled with screws. They rained out on the floor.

"We are so hopeless," I laughed, looking at the mess.

"Defeat makes me hungry," Mikey said, pushing Cripple's cardboard casket away. "Let's get food."

We went to the Vending Machine down the hall, looking to make a selection from the tastiest-looking coin-op.

"The problem with the Vending Machine," Mikey said, examining the elaborate Rube Goldberg–like chain-reaction machines that the Tinkers and Gearheads designed for their sponsors, "is that after all the marbles roll through their chutes and trigger all the music box mechanisms or whatever . . . like, after the hamster wheel powers the conveyor belt and drops your purchase in your hand, all the magic is gone. It's just corporate candy and the only thing left to do is eat it. Boring."

"You make a very unconvincing argument," I teased. "Since when do you not want to eat Javajacks?"

"Was I talking about Javajacks? Javajacks don't count." He swiped his card to release a coin token and dropped it in the slot. A box of the stuff slid down retro Hot Wheels® tracks, bounced on a trampoline, and fell through a basketball hoop. "Eating these are *even better* than the hype." He poured a handful in his mouth. "But I still need to get real food," he said, his words muffled by chocolate and caffeine crunches.

We logged out of the DIY Depot and took the escalator down to Culture Shock. While passing the third floor Pure Science rooms, I saw Eva Bloom and Palmer Phillips leaving Cosmonova together. The nature documentaries they showed on the domed screen of Cosmonova were nothing compared to the nature shows that went on in the seats. Kids usually just went there to make out.

"What was Rocket's boyfriend doing with Eva Bloom in Cosmonova?" I asked, but it was almost a rhetorical question. Everyone knew.

Mikey laughed and mimed a gesture that could be interpreted as eating a burrito. Except it wasn't.

"Quit being obscene," I snapped at him. I was about to intouch® Ari with the news of potential cheat-code evidence, but I didn't.

I didn't want to start a big rumor riot, but I hoped for Rocket's sake that Palmer and Eva both just had an unadvertised interest in images from the Hubble space telescope.

Down in Culture Shock, I waited in line with Mikey. He spent the whole time telling dirty jokes about Team Player sponsors.

I wanted to tell him, *Hey, guess what? I'm getting branded. Implausible, right?* But I couldn't really come up with a way to say it that didn't sound like a betrayal.

"Hey, where're you going?" he asked when I started to

walk away before the punchline, which probably was something about "getting branded in the locker room."

"I'm not in the mood for Mexican. I'm going to get a slice of pizza."

At the Little Italy counter, I pointed and mumbled, "Pepperoni, *grazie*." Then I went to find Mikey again, determined now to just get it said. But I got distracted.

"Look, it's them," I said, nudging him after he had finished insulting the Culture Shock staff in Spanish. Some of the staff looked annoyed, but others were impressed with his pronunciation and verb tense agreement.

"*¿Quiénes?*" he asked, picking up his burrito and Poke® cola and looking around.

I tried to be sly and point out Sophia and the guy I assumed was Elijah sitting at a table. "The Unidentified."

Mikey laughed at me. "Them? That's who you've got on your naughty list?" He started walking over to them.

"What're you doing?" I hissed, but followed after him.

"Hey, is it OK if we sit here?" Mikey said, already taking a seat beside Elijah and unwrapping his burrito. I stood there kind of awkwardly while Sophia looked me over.

"I'm sorry about the other day," I blurted out. "All the nosy questions, or whatever. I . . ." I didn't know how to finish my sentence.

"Yeah, it's true," Mikey said with his mouth full. "She's got some kind of condition. We've been to doctors, but there's nothing they can do." He took another bite. "She's beyond help."

"Shut up," I mumbled, and quickly took a seat. The acne-cheeked Elijah kept watching me, but I didn't trust myself to make eye contact.

I sort of stared at Sophia's plate while she ate her pizza. She pulled it apart like a buzzard—a hypersystematic, obsessive-compulsive buzzard. She piled the pepperoni into a wobbling tower, peeled off the cheese layer and folded it into a pile, careful to first scrape off the sauce into a glob to the side of her now-naked crust.

"I know you from somewhere," Mikey said looking at Elijah. "You race, right?"

"Yeah."

"But . . . you're not a Team Player?"

"No. I'm not." He reached over to take one of Mikey's nacho chips. "The last one to the finish line doesn't generally get a logo, the glory, or name-recognition." He licked the salt from his fingers and held out his hand. "I'm Elijah."

Mikey glanced at me, then took Elijah's hand in the awkwardly formal gesture. Elijah held on a little too long.

"Don't," Sophia warned, not looking up from her plate.

"I'm just being friendly," he said, leaning back in his chair now.

Elijah didn't seem to notice the elaborate ritual taking place on Sophia's plate. He was probably used to it. But I had to ask, "Why are you skinning your pizza?"

"I like to deconstruct my food into its composite parts when possible. There's an elemental purity to the act, and the essences of the ingredients are better appreciated separately."

"Oh." I watched her cut a small piece off her cheese heap and nibble it carefully.

"How do you eat soup?" Mikey asked.

"She hates soup." Elijah seemed amused.

"I don't hate it," Sophia said defensively. "I just don't trust it. I mean, what's it trying to hide?"

I took a bite of my pizza in the traditional way, weirded out that we were sitting here casually eating with suspected members of the Unidentified. And that they were just normal kids. Well, maybe not exactly *normal*. I eyeballed Sophia's dissected pizza slice, and listened to Elijah involve Mikey in a discussion about learning more through failure than success.

Then out of the buzz and chatter of conversation in Culture Shock, I heard one voice rise above others. A girl's voice, sharp: "What are you doing here, Cayenne? I thought you transferred to another site. Did you miss us too much?"

It was Quelly Atkins, terror general of the Fashion Fascists.

The sound of female laughter could be chilling. Anyone who thought girl-giggling was harmless, charming, and pink was way misguided. I pressed Record on my intouch® to capture the uniquely primate sound.

Cayenne was standing in line, trying to ignore the shrill voices.

"Those harpies," Elijah muttered.

"What?" Sophia said, taking a bite of her naked pizza crust and surveying the scene.

Quelly projected her voice so everyone could hear. "I heard you've been throwing yourself at Palmer again. Carving love notes to him and stuff. That's so psychotic." Quelly took another step closer and hissed something I couldn't hear.

Sophia got to her feet with a speed I didn't think she had in her. I watched, amazed, as Sophia used her bulk to clear a path right to the Fashion Fascists. She grabbed Quelly Atkins's arm and spun her around.

Quelly looked shocked that someone touched her. I was pretty surprised too. The Fashion Fascists always looked airbrushed and unreal, an illusion you would pass right through if you got too close.

"Don't touch me, freak!" Quelly shrieked.

"Believe me, I already regret it. I'll need to sanitize my hands with antibacterial wipes so they don't smell like jealousy-sweat and Chanel knockoff all day."

Quelly stood there with her mouth open, unable to say a word. The other foot soldiers took up the fight.

"You pushy cow, we weren't talking to you," the little blond one said.

"Yeah, what's your problem? Are you premenstrual? You look really bloated," Ashleah Carter said, pinching the roll of flesh around Sophia's middle.

They continued on like that for, like, ever. Making fun of Sophia's elaborately shaved eyebrows and dull-gray metal braces. And Sophia just stood there and took it, not even blinking at their mosquito buzzing and blood sucking.

Elijah had disappeared to help Cayenne leave the scene while the Fashion Fascists' attention was on bigger things.

Protecht security finally swooped in to break it up. Quelly turned on the charm, laughing and saying they were only playing. I don't think they bought it, but Sophia shrugged and headed back to our table.

She sat back down and popped a single slice of pepperoni in her mouth, and looked around Culture Shock, humming.

Mikey and I were staring at her, astonished.

"Ho shit," Mikey said.

I nodded. "I've never seen anyone get in the way of the Fascists like that before."

Sophia just shrugged. "Well, if you deconstruct Quelly Atkins into her composite elements, she's not much more than equal parts jealousy and insecurity, acrylic fingernails, and a chemical composition of peroxide and amino compounds to get that dye-bottle red hair. See? Not so scary."

"Yeah, but *you're* pretty scary," I mumbled. "I'd hate for you to deconstruct me. What did Cayenne do to get the Fascist wrath like that?"

Sophia stuck her finger in her pizza sauce and licked it. "Cayenne has her secrets, and her reasons for keeping them."

Up in the Studio, I couldn't hear the music the way I usually did. Listening for what was missing and not what was there.

"So who's this Murdoch guy Mr. Levy is always talking about?" Mikey asked, messing around with some amplifier cords. "Hey, are you OK?"

"Yeah. No. I don't know."

"Well, that pretty much covers the spectrum of human emotion, then."

My lip twitched into a not-quite smile. "Listen to this."

I had copied over the laughter recordings I'd been collecting on my intouch® and saved the file as *Last Laugh*. Laughter was . . . acoustically extreme. The sounds people made jumped around in pitch, and effortlessly hit high notes far beyond opera singer range. I wanted to rearrange the tones into a melody.

I'd been listening to these laugh tracks, but there was nothing funny about them. Especially the final track, the one I'd just recorded in Culture Shock. It gave me chills.

"What does it sound like Quelly said to her?" I passed the headphones to Mikey.

He listened. Then he backed up the sequence and listened again.

"'Don't deny. You know you wanted it'?" Mikey said, tossing the headphones back to me. "I don't know. These headphones are substandard."

"Yeah," I said, staring at the control board. "Why do you think she came back? Cayenne?"

"What?"

"Ari said she didn't know why the Fascists dropped her—"

"You could fill a fifteen-terabyte disc with what Ari doesn't know."

"Hey, that's my best friend you're talking about," I snapped back.

Mikey put his hands up defensively. "Yeah, well, maybe she should act like it sometime."

The practice session pretty much sucked after that. We logged out early from the Studio. It was almost closing time anyway. Ari buzzed, wanting to know if I needed a ride home.

kidzero: it's ok. my mom's picking me up. @ARI

I couldn't tell her I was getting branded over the intouch®. And I didn't want to admit it, but after what she said to me when I told her about Jeremy checking out my page, I was afraid she wouldn't believe me without proof. Maybe Mikey was right. I shouldn't be afraid of telling my best friend something important, right?

After this meeting with the administrators, she'd know the whole story soon enough.

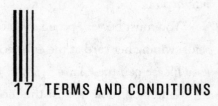

17 TERMS AND CONDITIONS

Winterson met Mom at the entrance and gave her a temporary ID to enter the Game after all the players had logged out. There were a bunch of security measures in place that made sure adults couldn't get into the Game sites. Even though it was inconvenient, these precautions comforted Mom.

"Did you have a hard time getting off work?" I asked her. "Sorry for the trouble."

I could tell that Mom had fixed her hair and makeup for the meeting. She didn't look like herself. She looked happy. "Don't be silly," she told me, attempting to fix my hair. "I've been hoping to get a call like this for a long time." She hugged me around the shoulders. Whispered that she was "so proud" before pulling away.

Seriously, who was this woman?

"It's so nice and quiet in here," Mom said as Winterson led us through the empty Pit.

I rolled my eyes, but I guess very few adults ever really saw the Game in action, in all its overstimulating glory of *interaction*.

"You must be very proud of Katey, Ms. Dade," Winterson said, swiping her card at the entrance to headquarters.

"Please call me Claire."

Winterson took us past the reception desk, down a hall toward the administrators' office. I had never been back here before. The halls had windowed walls, some of the blinds were drawn, but in some you could see offices. There were logos of different sponsors on each of the doors. Some of the cool hunters were packing up to go home, but a lot of them were still at their desks reviewing video footage and talking on phones.

The Game was super kid-centric, marketed as a place where we could devise our own schedules and do things at our own pace. Sometimes you could go a whole day and see only three adults. It was weird to think that there was a whole business working here behind the scenes that we never saw.

Winterson pressed a buzzer and waited for a click before she pushed open the door.

"Dr. Grant? Mrs. Bond?" Winterson said, hovering in the foyer. "Katey Dade and her mother are here to discuss terms and conditions."

"Dear Google, that makes this whole ordeal sound overly ceremonious," Mrs. Bond said with a breezy laugh, welcoming us in. "This is a cause for celebration."

She extended a hand to me, and waved away my advisor. "Good game, Katey," she said. Then she greeted my mom with a friendly "Vivyan. It's a pleasure."

I'd only seen the administrators at Newbie Orientation in the first week of Level 13–17. Mrs. Vivyan Bond looked exactly the same as she did on screen. She had no problems playing up the Bond-girl references bloggers were always geeking about. Her eyebrows were precision-plucked to give her a constant expression of amused indifference.

"Dr. Grant is sitting with your potential sponsors in the other room, Katey. They're excited to meet you."

Sponsors, plural? I looked over at my mom. She seemed as newbie-shook about this whole thing as I was.

We were led to a conference room. My potential sponsors—a retired cop–looking man and a young woman with a fairybelle haircut—were hunched over the glass-topped conference table. They were peering down through the glass, watching images projected from below. Dr. Grant shut off the video stream quickly when he saw my mom and me approaching, but I saw they'd been watching the Unidentified video. I'd seen it so many times, I knew every second of it.

"Here they are," Dr. Grant said, clapping his hands twice like two exclamation points. "Please, have a seat. Both of you."

He arranged it so that Mom sat beside the retired-cop guy, and I had a seat by the pixie-faced cool hunter.

"Hi, Kid," she said cheerfully as I tried to get comfortable in the strangely designed armchair. "I'm Anica Lass from Trendsetters clothing."

Trendsetters clothing wanted to brand me? I looked down at what I was wearing. I had on a T-shirt that Mikey had doodled on when he was bored in Lecture Hall last year. There were drawings of little birds pooping on my shoulder. This was not exactly the Trendsetters "look."

"Kidzero," the older man barked at me after introducing himself to my mom. I jumped and leaned around Anica to look at him. "Harrison," he said reaching out his hand. "Site security supervisor for Protecht Securities." He had a burly, grandpa-ish quality . . . but he held my hand a bit too long. I wondered if it was a psychological tactic to make me feel uncomfortable, because if it was, it worked.

Anica was on her feet, introducing herself to my mom and admiring the cut of Mom's skirt. "Very flattering," she said, smiling like a cheerleader who volunteered at an animal shelter.

"This is such an exciting occasion," Mrs. Bond announced after we had settled back in our seats. "Matching our players up with appropriate sponsors is one of the most rewarding parts of our duties as administrators."

The administrators went on to explain the school's history of partnership and cooperation with approved sponsors, and outlined the benefits of having a company invested in a child's education. She cited studies of players performing better and getting higher scores. "So you see there is tangible value in the partnership, not simply increased social capital." I was kind of drifting off, but mostly because it was obvious they were speaking to my mom and not me.

Then the brand representatives did their spiel. Again, more for my mom's benefit than for mine. Although Anica did look at me when she described the new Trendsetters wardrobe I'd be supplied with if I agreed to sign.

"Isn't that wonderful, Kiddie?" Mom beamed at me, before turning her attention back to Anica. "I've always wanted her to wear nicer clothes. It's just hard to budget it in and keep the credits balanced."

I focused all my undeveloped powers of mind-control on Anica, pleading with her not to mention the purchases I'd made with Ari.

"I completely understand," Anica assured her. Though it was hard to imagine how she could. In the big ocean of life experiences, my mom was drowning. And maybe I was wrong, but it didn't look like Anica ever even got her hair wet.

Anica just winked at me while mom scrolled through the latest spring collection. They huddled together, picking out clothes they thought I would look "adorable" in.

Mom smiled. "It's all the things I'd always wished I could give you, Kiddie."

Anica put her hand on Mom's shoulder. "You don't have to worry about that anymore, Claire. You've done so, so much for your daughter, this is something we can take care of for the both of you." She looked at me. "I promise you, Kid. Things are going to get a lot easier for you now. For both of you."

Relief glittered in mom's eye.

"Mom, cut it out," I said softly, but it felt like I was choking on something. I'd never seen my mom so happy.

Mom also seemed really impressed with Harrison's play-by-play of what Protecht Securities provided for the Game as a whole and its sponsored students particularly. "In addition to the GPS and intouch® response system available to all players, which alerts the authorities to potential dangers both in and outside the Game, our young agents work closely with us to develop new security measures. They enjoy a level of access to protective services and are provided with personal guidance to navigate ethical concerns and safety situations."

Dr. Grant briefly outlined the changes that would be made to my Network status and the onsite benefits of being on the It List. He pulled up a textual agreement for us to scroll through on the glass table. He finished with "Any questions?"

"Sounds like an amazing opportunity. Doesn't it, Kiddie?" She was so excited, and I definitely didn't want to let her down, but I couldn't stop feeling that they must've made a mistake.

"Why me, though?" I asked everyone in the room. "Why did you choose me out of all the kids in the school? What do you expect me to do?"

Anica laughed. "I know, it's all probably overwhelming, but you don't need to worry. We chose you because you had an eye for the cutting-edge, so actually, all we expect from you is for you to be yourself. And share your content with us, if applicable. We won't ask you to do anything you're not comfortable with."

"You've shown a special talent in extracurricular investigations," Harrison said cryptically, obviously preferring not to mention the Unidentified in front of my mom. "The kind of talents we tend to keep a close eye on under any circumstances." His lip twitched in a kind of hidden warning. "In any case, we're very pleased that young Jeremy recommended you to us. He expressed a deep interest in getting the chance to work together with you."

Jeremy said that?

Mrs. Bond set a fingerprint-scanning touchpad in front of my mom. She made a valiant effort at reading the glowing print, but I could tell she was skimming the end.

Harrison, then Anica, slid the touchpad over to my side of the table. I still had questions about what would be expected of me, but whatever it was, it had to be worth all the benefits I was about to get in this arrangement.

I scrolled quickly through the text.

Then clicked OK.

18 PRIVATE MESSAGES

I couldn't believe it. It probably didn't feel real because I hadn't told Ari yet, so when I got home I opened my notebook® to send her a private message. But I noticed I had a new message in my inbox and opened it.

> Congratulations. You have joined the ranks of the sold souls. Hope you got a good deal for the price you paid. *by anonymous*

I was more pissed off than scared this time. I was about to fire off a demanding *who are you?* email, but I didn't click Send. In all the stranger-danger seminars they said I should never respond to people I didn't know, but that's not what made me pause. I read the message again. Three times. News of the branding still hadn't been made public. Jeremy knew about it from his sponsors, now *our* sponsors. So this person had access to parts of my record that only administrators and sponsors could see.

And there was something familiar about the cadence of the words. The language. It was him.

I wrote:

I know who you are. I recognize your voice.
by kidzero

I felt a little dizzy after I sent it, maybe because I had been holding my breath. A new message pinged and the air rushed out of me like a deflating balloon.

You shouldn't be talking to strangers anyway.
Who am I?
by anonymous

I didn't really know his name or anything about him, but I couldn't admit that now. I wanted to keep talking to him. I quickly typed:

You are the Unidentified. The Unidentified refuses
to be typecast, target-marketed, corporate-
identified, defined.
by kidzero

I didn't have to wait long for a response.

•—•

the UnID.

"Kiddie, what are you doing in there?"

"Nothing," I said, closing my notebook® quickly.

Mom opened my bedroom door. She was smiling. "Well, are you ready to go out and celebrate? Let me take you out to dinner at Aunt Gillie's."

"Yeah, sure," I said, feeling a little guilty. This was, like, my mom's worst fear, me chatting with strangers on the interweb, but I smiled back at her. My mind was a chemical rush of excitement from my little secret. I needed to find out who this guy was.

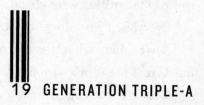

19 GENERATION TRIPLE-A

When I entered the Game the next day, my full attention snapped over to one of the advertisement screens in the Pit. It was showing the dummy suicide film. Right there on one of the sponsors' screens.

The film had been re-edited so instead of the long shots and slow music, it was cut up into choppy, out-of-sequence clips. The final splatter instant-replayed five or six times, intercut with the close-up of the balloon face. The text: WHO ARE YOU? CHOOSE YOUR IDENTITY. flashed on the screen in an edgy-looking font, followed by the logo for Trendsetters clothing.

I stared at the screen in shock. Did clicking OK give Trendsetters permission to remix the film just because it was linked from my page? I couldn't believe it. I didn't have the rights to that film.

Everything subversive about the Unidentified film had been spun to sell Trendsetter clothing. I wondered if I had an angry anonymous private message waiting for me now, or if the Unidentified were already planning ways to retaliate.

Everyone I passed was chattering about the ad spot.

"I was there when they were filming it! I can't believe our Game site is in a national campaign."

"I saw an original director's cut. But the remix is so much better."

"Look. It's her."

People I barely knew were pointing at me.

The hype was making me uncomfortable. Why was it getting so much attention now? Two days ago, no one had even blinked.

A new text buzzed into my intouch®.

aria: why didn't you tell me? @KID

Oh no. Ari. I didn't think news would spread so fast. I thought I'd have time to tell her everything before it went live.

Ari's Network page told me where she was "right now," and I hurried up to the Sweatshop.

I found her sitting on a sofa with her advisor Jaye. Jaye's hair was cotton-candy pink, and her eyeliner looked like Ari had done it for her.

"I'll let you girls talk," Jaye said, standing up. "Come by my office if you need *anything*, Aria." Jaye pronounced her name the way Ari liked.

Ari's violet contact lenses were shimmering with tears.

She swiveled her notebook® toward me so I could see the screen. On top of my Network page, the Trendsetter logo and Protecht Securities name were in a banner that read: PROUD SPONSORS OF KATEY DADE.

"How did that even happen?" she said, her voice rising.

"I don't know," I mumbled. "It all happened really fast." I told her about what a fluke it all had been, that they used my first search hit and continued interest in that Unidentified film we'd found to tag me as a trendspotter.

"I'm sorry, Ari. I didn't plan any of this."

My intouch® buzzed. I checked it on impulse, even though I probably should've waited until we weren't in the middle of a supersensitive conversation.

#IT_List_serv: yr invited to a meet & greet at the VIP lounge. come on! @KID

"What is it?" Ari asked.

"Nothing," I answered automatically. "It's just a meeting."

Ari held out her hand for my intouch®. "No more secrets," she said. I watched her read my invite. "You should go," she said quietly.

"Yeah, I know." I stood up. "But we're cool, right?"

"Sure," she said, still sniffling. "I mean, it's not like you

155

purposefully screwed your friends over to get fame, right?"

"Right," I said carefully. I was relieved, but it still didn't seem fair. Ari had busted her ass all year to get branded, and I kind of fluked my way into the VIP Lounge. "I'm sorry, Ari."

WE ARE GENERATION TRIPLE-A. The slogan hung on the wall in an edgy font etched in metal. The tenets of the It List were *Articulation, Argumentation, and Association.* The lounge was supposed to be a place to meet and associate with other promising players. Generation Triple-A was also the marketing term assigned to us, the kids spawned after Generation X, Y, and Z. They had been the end of an era, we were the beginning. We were rewarded with a peppy, battery-operated generation moniker (AAA) in exchange for our promise to remember the brands that formed our dearest childhood memories. Those chosen to be on the It List prided themselves on being the voice of this generation.

The lighting must've been different in the VIP Lounge than in the rest of the Game. It made everyone look airbrushed and perfect, even better than the natural light coming in though the skylight.

The whole back wall of the lounge was a mirror, making the space feel crowded and infinite. I caught a glimpse of my reflection in the wall and it looked like I had been Photoshopped into the scene. Falsified evidence to make it look like I belonged with all these pretty people.

Eva Bloom was giggling and gossiping up front with the big-name crowd, trying to get the attention of Palmer Phillips, but he was too busy posing with Abercrombie Fletcher. Fletcher had been branded since birth—he'd kinda inherited it from his PR-Papa.

Getting linked with a brand was supposed to be like being backstage with an *Idol* band or something, but the whole scene felt pretty plastic to me. I'd never socialized with these people before and couldn't think of a thing I wanted to talk about with them now.

"Hi." A guy in a logo T-shirt holding a can of Liquid Crack® came and sat next to me. "What's *your* name?"

It was obvious he didn't go to school here. He was outside of the Game's demographic age by at least five years.

"Kid," I mumbled, arms crossed.

"Whoa! Great name. Can I get you a drink, Kid?" He held up a can of Liquid Crack®.

"No thanks, I'm cool."

"I'm sure you are," he said, tilting his head back, chugging his high-energy, no carb, caffeine cocktail. I could almost hear his heart seize.

"I like your style, Kid."

I winced, but I think he took it as a smile.

"It's true, you've got a real cool anti-style style. And that shoelace accessory?" He raised his can to my pocket, like he was toasting my "look." "Subtle. Nice."

"It's utilitarian," I said.

His face dropped in a look of surprise and pulled out a notebook®. "I've never heard of that brand, did they just launch?"

I smiled a polite, someone-please-save-me smile.

"So who are you here with? Who got you? It was Élan, wasn't it?" He glared at a good-looking guy, early twenties, surrounded by a herd of Fashion Fascists. "That slick bastard," he muttered into his drink. He smiled at me. "I would've liked to have been the first to brand you," he said, winking. "I'd brand you any day of the week."

Ugh, gross. Was he flirting with me?

"No. Um, Anica invited me?" I said, looking around, trying to find someone else to talk to. I was surprised to see Rocket sitting by herself at a table. In the Sweatshop, she was the sun all the Craftsters orbited around. Here, she was just a girl.

"Anica Lass?" the Liquid Crack® guy said almost reverently. "Wow. She hasn't been interested in anyone on site since last year's popularity implosion with what's-her-name. Pepper Lewis."

"Cayenne? She had been with Trendsetters?" I was kind of embarrassed about how greedy I was for gossip, but I really wanted to know this story.

Two hands grabbed my shoulders firmly and I heard a smooth voice say, "I'm sorry, can you excuse me? I need to borrow my friend for a moment."

The Liquid Crack® guy said, "Obviously, she's a hot commodity," and immediately swiveled to talk to the kid on the other side of him.

I turned around to see Tycho Williams standing in front of me. I'd never been this close to him and had about forty emotions battling on my face. Surprise. Awe. Shame. Fear.

I think my expression finally settled on dread.

"Good game cashing in that linked-to film for celebrity perks," he said. I couldn't tell if he was being sincere or sarcastic. He gestured to the glitzy room around us. "It was so worth it, no?"

I frowned. He thought I'd sold them out. "I didn't give them permission to use that film," I said a little too loudly. Then softer, "When I signed, they told me they wouldn't ask me to do anything I wasn't comfortable with. And they didn't. Ask, I mean."

A crease flickered in the smooth space between his eyebrows. "Business as usual," he muttered. He watched the room cautiously. "Take everything you think you already know and do a cost-benefit analysis before you sell your soul."

"Hey, don't act like you've never smudged the glass with your thumb," I said defensively. "You did the same thing to get in here."

"On the one hand, you're right. On that one, you're wrong."

He pointed to the balloon wristband I'd been wearing all this time. I covered it up, embarrassed, then guiltily pulled it off with a snap.

"I'm sorry," I choked out.

His teeth flashed white as he laughed it off. "Why are you apologizing to *me*?"

"Thought maybe you could pass it on? Tell the others I didn't mean for this to happen? Let them all know. Sophia. Lexie. Elijah . . . Cayenne."

His face lost its confident expression for a second.

"Yeah, yeah, yeah," he said, talking over me. "I'll spread the word if you *don't*."

"Sorry," I said again, not catching on until now that maybe the VIP Lounge wasn't the best place to be discussing the Unidentified.

"Yeah," he said, frowning.

Jeremy snaked his arm around my shoulders. "Hey, Kid," he said, then nodded to Tycho. "What were you two chatting on about?"

"Music production," I said without hesitation. Then I asked Tycho about mixing techniques I always wished I could discuss with him.

He answered without missing a beat and we talked for a bit before he excused himself.

"Be sly," Tycho said, then mingled back into the scene.

"Tycho Williams, huh?" Swift asked after he left.

"It's a meet-and-greet." I shrugged. "Besides, who *doesn't* know Tycho Williams. Why?"

He smiled and squeezed me tighter. "Just checking out my competition."

I didn't know how to answer. It was pretty surreal. Discussing music with Tycho Williams, flirting with Jeremy

Swift. It was almost like everything they ever said about the VIP Lounge was true.

"Hey, I just have a small announcement to make," Palmer said to the crowd, hopping up on a catwalk. Everyone got quiet and looked up to Palmer. The cool hunters who were working the room stood off to the side, admiring their choice of spokesman.

"I'd like to say a few words from our sponsors."

He went on about how Eva Bloom's sponsor, Kiss Off® lipstick, was going to hold some kind of kissing contest by the Park after the meeting. He mentioned the marketing campaign tagline: "If you're not man enough to kiss off this long-lasting lipstick, then Kiss Off®!"

"Trust me"—Palmer tousled his ironic haircut—"I can tell you from personal experience, you are not going to want to miss this event." He winked at Eva, sitting in the front row.

She licked her cherry-stained lips and looked back over her shoulder at the other Team Players all fidgety in their seats. Gross.

I shot a glance at Rocket to see how she was handling this announcement. It was disgusting. Kiss Off® was going to ride the rumors of Eva's reputation just as much as all the guys in there wanted to ride Eva. I was about to leave Jeremy and go and comfort her when Palmer jumped down from the stage.

"Hey! New recruit!" I saw Palmer Phillips playfully pushing past Abercrombie Fletcher to get closer to me.

"Sorry it took me so long to spot you. You already fit right in." He nodded to Jeremy's arm slung across my shoulders. "I usually take it as my solemn duties as spokesman to help the newly tagged get accustomed to life on the It List." He grinned magnificently. You could kind of tell how he got to be the top-ranked player on Network. He was definitely charming.

But his fang tooth gleamed a little too sharkily when he smiled, and I glanced uncomfortably over to the table where Rocket still sat alone. Had going out with her just been one of his duties as spokesman?

She watched him talking to me now, the hurt of being recently dropped still fresh on her face.

"It's quite a scene, eh?" Palmer said, spreading out his arms to embrace the preening mob of Fashion Fascists, the obnoxious Team Players, all looking like catalogue cut-outs.

I nodded, not trusting myself to say anything appropriate.

"Still, it's not all champagne soda pop and scene parties being It, you know?" Palmer confided in us. "There's some generics . . . jealous generics, I bet . . . targeting people on the List. It's getting out of hand. We shouldn't have to worry about snipers."

"Snipers?" Jeremy said, immediately interested.

"Yeah, someone vandalized Abercrombie Fletcher—"

"How do you vandalize a person?" I interrupted.

"Well, OK. They vandalized his jacket, but Abe really loves his jacket, you know? So yesterday some generics were shooting spit wads and stuff at him because someone had stenciled a bull's-eye and the words I AM A TARGET MARKET on his back."

"Any idea who did it?" Jeremy wanted to know.

"Yeah, have you ever heard of the Unidentified?" Palmer asked as if he were talking about an obscure buzz band.

I froze, and Jeremy shot a glance at me.

He nodded. "I've heard of them. What did you hear?"

"That they're this reckless antigroup with the best bad publicity since Kennedy Weiss got caught stealing those down-market jeans."

"So, you think they're . . . good? Even though they're taking shots at your best friend?" I asked, trying to work out what he meant.

"Oh, yeah. They're meffing genius."

20 KISS OFF

Mikey was in the Park, sweaty faced and picking fights with some final level danger jocks. The two hypertestosteroned adrenaline junkies looked like they were just barely tolerating Mikey.

"I'm modding a gravity bike, all from JunkYard spares. It's going to slide downgrade with nearly frictionless freefall," he was telling them.

"There's no way you're going to get any meaningful velocity in the Park," the weasel-looking guy cut him off. "And don't pretend you can get any speed off-site, junior. Four months to freedom," he said, bumping fists with his friend.

"You think I'm going to wait until I'm legal to trick off

campus?" Mikey argued. "My bones are so supple now. I'm not going to weenie out and squander my superhealing powers waiting for permission to ride."

"Keep talking," the guy with the physique of a fridge warned.

"Yeah, I'd stick to butt-boarding, son," the other one said dismissively.

"Mikey!" I hissed, doing a frantic *c'mere* gesture.

Mikey waved back distractedly and ignored me. He kept insulting the two older players like he had a death wish.

I hopped down into the showroom and grabbed Mikey's arm. "What are you doing?"

He shook me off. "Discussing breeze with these meaty gentlemen here."

The lean-looking blond guy who recommended butt-boarding as a suitable pastime flipped him off.

"I need to talk to you," I said.

"Hey, you're the Suicide Pit girl," the blond guy said, pointing at me. "We were just talking about ways to re-create the stunt without the dummy."

"Yeah, and minus the splat. Ideally," the big guy said, squishing his hands together.

"Sounds more real than real, right?"

"Sounds like literal suicide, actually," I said, then saw Mikey stalking out of the showroom.

"So do you know them?" the beefier of the two asked me, getting closer. "Do you know who they are? The Unidentified?"

"I . . ." I saw Mikey leaving the Park. "I have to go. And, um, don't die. Okay?"

The guys hooted in celebration as if dying would be the most authentic outcome of their adventure. I wondered if I should let Harrison and Protecht know to keep an eye on them. You never knew with adrenaline junkies.

"Mikey, wait. What's going on?"

"Since when did you decide to be BFFs with brands?" he said, spinning around. "Was this Ari's idea?"

"No. She didn't . . ." I could kind of understand why Ari was upset about me getting branded, but I didn't think Mikey would make such a big deal out of it. I was prepared for some teasing, but not this. "Mikey, what's wrong?"

"Guess," he said. "You saw what happened with Ari— and she only got cliqued with the Craftsters. You're *branded* now, Kid. Do you even know what that means?"

"It doesn't mean . . . This doesn't change anything." I laughed. "It's not going to change *me*."

"Right," he said dully. "And you weren't just partying in the VIP Lounge with Jeremy Swift." He walked away.

A bass-heavy remix thundered in from just outside the Park. Hooting, whistle-shrieks, and man-shouts razored through the speaker-shaking noise. That Kiss Off® promo contest Palmer had announced was getting started. On a huge screen, Eva was applying product to her pouty lips. There was already a line forming.

I tried to find Mikey in the crowd.

My intouch® buzzed.

swiftx: you going to after hours tonight? @KID

I froze, focusing on the words on the tiny screen. Was Jeremy asking me out? After Hours were these big Friday night events held in the Game after closing time. Ari had been trying to convince me to go since she got cliqued, but I'd never gone before. Partly because my mom didn't like the idea of me being out late, and partly because I wasn't interested in the *Idol* bands usually scheduled to play.

Up on-screen, Eva was making out with Team Players who had been lured out of the Park. She swapped spit with the more popular players, and smooched the other generics quickly before pushing them away. Her lipstick did remain impossibly in place.

I didn't want to watch this anymore.

I felt my intouch® more than heard it.

swiftx: come with me. @KID

kidzero: ok. @SWIFT

I searched for a path out of the mob and saw Ari standing with Rocket and the other Craftsters in the back watching the spectacle, disgusted too.

Slut, Ari mouthed. And I glanced back at Eva Bloom. Ari had always had a "no empathy" policy for Fashion Fascists. But I felt kind of sorry for her, up there getting mauled by males to sell lipstick to hostile girls.

I got a reply. I thought it would be Jeremy, but it came from Mikey.

mikes: have fun. @KID

Did that mean Mikey had seen me tell Swift I would go to After Hours with him? I couldn't quite identify the feeling I had in my gut just then, but if I had to guess, it would be related to some species of eel.

I turned to see Mikey up on the screen, leaning in toward Eva. He looked like he was taking the Kiss Off® challenge literally, making determined efforts to suck the product from her lips.

The crowd laughed and cheered.

The eel feeling in my stomach twitched electric and stopped my heart.

21 HIGH PROFILE

It destroyed me to see him up there, stupid and insensitive just like any of the typical guys in the Game. I pushed my way out of the crowd, feeling so disappointed in him and . . . injured, I guess.

Worse was, I couldn't let it show. Everyone was watching me. I was branded now. I had stream-groupies. People were whispering about how Jeremy and I were linked. That we were a thing.

I felt completely unprepared for all the attention I was suddenly getting.

#pro_harrison: you're scheduled for security procedures review. 14.20. use VIP entrance @KID

I asked someone in the VIP Lounge where I was supposed to go to meet my sponsors and she showed me to a door in back with a swipe-card lock. The little light flashed green when I swiped, and the door opened up to the hall of offices I'd seen in headquarters. The rush from having full access didn't feel like freedom, more like that any second I was going to get caught.

I found the door with the new Protecht logo. They had used the picture I'd taken after the Unidentified rearranged the surveillance cameras into a creepy-intimate embrace to get past security. Apparently, corporate identity designers weren't afraid of irony.

I knocked. Harrison was sitting at a desk with only a simple-screen computer, but all around him the place was wired with surveillance screens showing the rooms and passages on the different floors. Harrison's attention seemed to be focused mainly on the Kiss Off® contest wrapping up outside of the Park.

He pulled out a seat for me and, without even saying hello, launched into a security briefing.

"This is stuff you should already know," he grumbled. "Don't give out personal information to non–administration approved sites, don't leave your notebook® unattended. And don't feed the trolls."

I nodded.

"Also, never give out your password to anyone else. Not your best friend, not your boyfriend." He paused and gave me an uncharacteristic wink. "Well, in your case, it's probably okay for you to give it to your boyfriend. Jeremy's a good kid."

I swallowed, embarrassed. Not only because granddad Harrison seemed to believe the rumors about my love life, but I was afraid that he would find out that Ari and I had exchanged passwords forever ago.

He continued on with his lecture. "Again, safety precautions you should already know. I can't tell you how much energy we put into preventing hacker attacks only to have silly girls leave their notebooks® open for any charmer."

I was offended by his "silly girls" remark, but didn't say anything. I glanced at one of the screens running on his desk. What looked like intouch® comments scrolled endlessly down the display. I wondered which streams Protecht was subscribed to. By the amount of activity update, it looked like all of them. But there was no way Protecht could follow every update made on site. Right?

"You're branded now. And you're branded by the finest security and protection company in the market. You must exercise caution at all times. We can't afford embarrassing leaks."

I wondered why Protecht even bothered branding me if they thought I was such a liability.

"Now, as part of the agreement you've made with Protecht Securities, we'd really appreciate it if you used your particular skills to help us with fact-finding missions to improve the security in the Game." He scrolled through a list on his screen. "What do you know about . . ."

I prepared myself to deny knowing anything about the Unidentified.

"Alibi," he said.

"What?"

"There's a program kids are installing on their intouches® that allows them to input false GPS coordinates."

"Oh." Oh shit. That's the program Tesla said Elle Rodriguez had created.

"Yeah, you see the problem with that," he said, misreading the panic on my face. "If we don't have accurate information as to the whereabouts of players we can't effectively protect them."

"Of course," I said. "I'll . . . um . . . listen for any word about that." I wished I were a more skillful liar.

"These unauthorized programs are no joking matter. Players think they're being sneaky passing around a harmless tracker app to their friends. But it's just the perfect cover to spread wormy malware. It's Protecht's job to find these bugs and squash them."

I thought of the creepy eyeball icon pulsing on my notebook® and how quickly it had disappeared. Had I been infected by some kind of maggot code? Did he already know I had that app installed on my page?

"Is there anything else that has come to your attention in the past few days?" Harrison asked, examining my face.

What, you mean like a list of individuals suspected of dropping paint bombs in the Pit, holding Illegal Arts Workshops on how to get around Network security, and vandalizing It Listers' clothing to use them as target practice? No.

"Yes," I blurted out, afraid of what he might find hidden if I didn't give him something. "There were some guys in the Park today talking about recreating the dummy drop prank for real."

Harrison clapped his hands and it sounded like a gunshot. "I knew it! I told that little trendsetting pixie of yours it was a mistake to give more exposure to that film. 'All subversive elements will be removed,' she said." He was talking fast now, pacing around the room. "She doesn't understand how impressionable you kids can be." He pointed a fat finger at me. "Who are they?"

"Who?"

"The boys in the Park."

"I . . . I'm sorry. I didn't get their names. I didn't know—"

He grabbed the back of my chair and slid me over to his desk, in front of his screen.

He pulled up a program.

"What's this?" I asked, staring at the screen.

"Profile," Harrison grumbled. "It allows us to do more detailed demographic searches based on physical criteria."

Harrison asked me questions about the boys' eye color, hair styles, height, age, body type, race.

"They were Level Seventeens, I'm sure."

Harrison inputted all their details, and found a match with their names on Network.

"Are these the guys?" Harrison asked, pulling up Game ID photos on the screen.

173

I was so amazed by the program, interested to see how it worked, that I barely realized what I was doing. I was about to hand their identities over to Protecht just because they were bragging about some crazy stunt they may or may not have the guts to pull off.

"Well?"

I didn't know how to turn back now without raising suspicion, so I nodded.

"Okay, Mr. Kimo Kauwe and Mr. Derek Ennis," Harrison said, going in as admin and flagging their Network pages. Putting marks on their record that they would never see. "We've got our eyes on you."

I breathed in sharply. That first private message. The voice of the Unidentified.

"Can anyone use Profile?" I asked, trying to sound casual.

He watched me carefully and asked, "Why?"

Because I wanted to see if I could use it to find out more about the leader of the Unidentified, I thought. I blinked my eyes, opened them wide and did my best impression of Quelly Atkins. "I know so many people who would love to try it out. It's almost like building a SimKid! It would revolutionize dating technology."

He just stared at me. "It's not for public use."

"Too bad. It would be such a high-volt matchmaker." I played with my hair for added Quelly emphasis.

"Silly girls," Harrison muttered.

"You watch out," a musical-sounding voice called out from the hall. Both Harrison and I swiveled toward it.

Anica stood in the doorway, smirking. "Underestimate a girl and she'll take full advantage." She pushed away from the wall. "Kid, when you're finished chatting with the man, come by and see me, okay?"

She waved to Harrison and continued down the hall. His face had a pinkish color now, I couldn't tell if it was anger or embarrassment or what.

"Are we done?" I asked cautiously.

He waved me away, and I made my escape.

Anica welcomed me into her office. She was sipping a blue-colored beverage through a straw and looking out her window. A window that looked in on the VIP Lounge.

"How're you settling in to branded life, Kid?"

I didn't know how to reply to that without sounding ungrateful. "It's different," I mumbled.

"But are you?"

"Am I what?"

"Different." She clinked her glass down on her desk and took a seat.

"I don't think so."

"Do you know why we branded you, Katey?"

"'To provide me with opportunities only available from the dedication and investment of a caring sponsor,'" I quoted monotonously from her Terms and Conditions spiel.

"You're not like your mother," she said simply. I think she meant it as a compliment, but I was offended. Anica wasn't anything like how she had been when speaking with my mother either. "No, we branded you because we hoped for your authentic insights. We're looking to branch out," She smiled. "Expand our markets . . ."

She lifted her glass to the people out the window, laughing animatedly in the VIP Lounge, unaware of being watched—or hyperaware of being watched; it was hard to tell sometimes.

"The previous model of partnering with kids who have reached their height of popularity by doing the things they ought to do and buying the things they ought to buy hasn't given us the results we're looking for."

I thought of Ari, every calculated step she took to get the attention of the cool hunters.

"You mean like Cayenne Lewis?"

Anica nearly choked. "Oh, yes. That was a PR night-mare. She had the most perfect statistics, looked so good on screen. It was such a shame." She wagged her finger at the window. "That Palmer Phillips. Such a heartbreaker."

He was sitting at a booth in the lounge laughing with Abe Fletcher, trying to pull Eva Bloom into his lap.

"No. As much fun as it is courting the top players, it's like . . . advertising to the stockholders. You know? No. We want to be relevant to the tough customers. The disenfran-chised, dissenting voices of your generation."

"Why?"

"Because being a rebel never goes out of style." She smiled. "So, Katey. What more can you tell me about your friends the Unidentified?"

22 BEST FRIENDS FOREVER

I managed to leave the Trendsetter office without revealing anything about the Unidentified, mostly because I didn't really *know* anything about the Unidentified. Anica seemed to think that I was friends with them, and I was afraid to correct her. If the truth came out, Mom would be so disappointed that I couldn't manage to stay branded for one single day.

I went up to the Sweatshop to see Ari. She would know about these kinds of things, whether the sponsors could just end my contract because I was a bigger loser than they thought.

"You coming over to Ari's to get ready for After Hours?" Tesla asked me when I entered, not caring that those intouch® comments from Swift were supposed to be a private conversation.

I leaned over the arm of the sofa to see Tesla poking diodes into molded-polymer beads. Her blond hair was styled with elaborate braids, making a perfect Fibonacci spiral on the top of her head.

"Oh. I didn't know that was the plan."

The needle of Ari's machine went silent. "Yeah, everyone's coming over around seven," she said.

"OK. Good game," I said.

The sewing machine motor whirred as the needles stabbed the fabric.

"Jeremy Swift." Rocket said his name like a statement. "How did *that* happen?"

She and Ari exchanged a glance, and I didn't know what to say.

"He was, like, *on* you in the VIP Lounge," she said, putting the finishing touches on her needlepoint project. She was stitching the quote: *There is a special place in hell for women who don't help other women* surrounded by embroidered flames and sexy pinup devils. "It was like he was claiming you or something. Kid, you need to watch out for those super-possessive boys. Believe me, I know."

Oh, you mean like Palmer, who barely even looks at you in the VIP Lounge anymore?

I felt like a supersized jerk for even thinking that, but I was annoyed that she needed to say shit about Jeremy to make herself look better in front of the Craftsters.

"Aw, I think they look cute together," Tesla said. "I mean, I know he's technically a meatpounder and therefore deserves no praise from any self-respecting Princess, but full points for that pull, Kid."

Ari just continued sewing.

"I always thought you and Littleton had something going on," Avery said, breaking the yarn of her knit project with her teeth. "Showing up at After Hours with his best friend is quite the dagger-twist, don't you think?"

"What? No," I said louder than I meant to. The scene from the Kiss Off® contest flashed like a subliminal blip. "Jeremy's not his best friend. *I'm* his best friend."

Ari shook her fashionably too-long bangs and muttered, "Best friend. Right."

She released a slip of brown material from the torture of the sewing machine, held it against her body and admired the reflection of her newly fashioned slip dress.

What was I going to wear to After Hours? "Can I get a ride home to pick up some stuff before I come over?"

Ari didn't take her eyes off the mirror when she answered. "Oh. Sorry. I have a lot to do before tonight. Can't." She fake-pouted. "Sorry."

"Yeah. It's okay."

I guess I would have to take the shuttle home, then try to convince Mom to take me to Ari's. I'd say I was counting down the weeks until I turned sixteen, but I wasn't deluded enough to think that I'd be getting access to a car for my birthday.

"I can take you, Kid." Tesla was packing up her project.

"Thanks," I said. Tesla was always a sweetheart, but I was still surprised she volunteered to chauffeur me around all afternoon. Maybe it was just another hidden perk of being branded now.

Tesla held her card up against the dash and the motor purred to life.

"I still can't believe your folks didn't activate *any* restrictions on your ride."

"Just because the technology is available doesn't mean they've got to use it," she said, checking her mirrors. "Besides, I think they secretly like it when I come home and tell them about my day without GPS spoilers. If they'd preprogrammed my routes, all my adventures would have no entertainment value."

She maneuvered her car out of the massive parking lot, singing unselfconsciously to herself. Her singing voice was huskier than her speaking voice. It was a nice surprise.

"So. How's branded life?" she said casually.

I'd suspected it, but was a little disappointed to have it confirmed that Tesla was being friendly because of a change in my record.

I shrugged. I honestly didn't know how to answer. A lot had changed, but I still felt the same.

"Did you know they wanted to brand me?" she said, signaling left. "A couple times, actually."

"Who?"

"I don't want to name-drop," she said. "Doesn't really matter."

"Why didn't you click OK?"

"Did you *read* those terms and conditions?"

"Almost?"

She laughed. "Yeah, no one does. But I didn't think it was a good deal. I didn't want to give away the rights to my content and inventions, for what? Some free shit? To hang out in the VIP Lounge or whatever?"

"I should introduce you to Tycho Williams."

"Damn. Yes, please." She honked the horn in three short bursts for emphasis. "If I knew getting some branded boys would be part of the deal, I probably would've reconsidered."

I didn't answer at first. I didn't really want to admit how big a factor Jeremy had been in my decision to get on the It List.

Then her tone got serious. "And if I had known that the sponsors I declined would challenge every new design I came up with . . . " She punctuated her sentence with a frustrated animal growl. "Sore losers, for real."

"Is that why you're getting harassed for your flip-streams?"

"Indeed. If I drove over to their corporate headquarters and spent the night nailing all the office furniture to the ceiling to really flip their shit up, would you be my alibi?"

She laughed. But I froze at the word "alibi."

"Tess," I said quietly. "About Alibi . . . there's no, um,

contaminated code in that program or anything, is there?"

"No way. Elle crafted that app. It's sparkling sterile. Completely safe for consumption."

I told her about Protecht and their investigations into Alibi. "Just tell her to be stealthy. And to watch her back."

"You too."

I smiled, "I'm protected by the Protech logo. What do I have to be worried about?"

But Tesla still looked unconvinced. "There's been talk around the Sweatshop."

"There's always talk around the Sweatshop." I sighed.

"I know." She hesitated. "And I don't really want to add to the talking-behind-people's-backs. . . . But Ari and Rocket?"

"Yeah?"

"They're talking. So just be careful."

Ari lived in a nice house in a nice neighborhood. I'd been in this nice house so many times over the years that I knew everything about this place.

I knew the exact blooming schedule for the synthetic seeds in the front lawn. Mrs. Knowland made sure the grass was purple this time of year because she could. She was proud of how her landscaping made the natural oranges of the neighbors' oak trees look cheap. Not that Mrs. Knowland spent much time personally enjoying her yard. She always selected the "English garden in spring" view on her touch-screen kitchen window.

Everything was familiar at Ari's place, but never really comfortable. My cheeks always hurt a little bit from my strained smile. I can almost understand why Ari went around looking for drama and tragedy. It was painful to be perfect all the time.

Ari opened the door when I rang. She had a huge smile on her face that shrank a little when she saw me.

"Oh, hey," she said, not exactly unfriendly. "I thought you were Rocket. Hey, Tesla."

"Hello, Kid," Mrs. Knowland called from the kitchen. "Congratulations. We saw your name on the It List updates. Imagine our surprise."

"Uh, thanks."

"I was planning on redesigning Merilee's front room in opulent eggplant on Tuesday," she continued. "Please tell me you can get the workers to deliver the stone work by seven."

"I . . . don't," I stammered.

"She's not talking to you," Ari said, impatiently maneuvering us toward the staircase, past the showcase of all the gifts Mr. Knowland brought back for Ari from his conference trips.

"I don't care," Mrs. Knowland said to the phony flowers in the hall. "They need to get it done."

I followed Ari upstairs.

The walls of Ari's bedroom were wallpapered with posters and magazine pages. The layer was so thick that the room was probably completely soundproofed by now, which was good because the girls had the music up loud.

Ari never took down old posters, she just put her new interests up over them. Imagine the history you could read on those walls, like growth rings on a tree.

The latest layer on the surface now looked a lot like her Network profile page: Ari's favorite *Idol* band, manga drawings from her Japanese e-pal, crafty fashion spreads, the cover of *Times* featuring the vice president and her "controversial" hairstyle.

And speaking of controversial hairstyles, I soon found myself sitting on the bed while Ari tugged and twirled my limp and lifeless hair. She had bobby pins between her lips, so her voice was kind of muffled.

"OK. Now there's no escape. You are going to get *made*!"

"Yeah, you could be so pretty, Kid," Kasi said, looking wide-eyed at herself in the mirror. All I heard was *You're not pretty now.*

"Do you think they'll be done in time?" Ari asked Tesla distractedly as she pulled on my hair. I turned my head to see what Tesla was doing. She was on the floor soldering wires or something.

"Hold still," Avery said, blocking my view of Tesla. She had a tube of way red lipstick in one hand, and tilted my face up to her with the other. My natural instinct would've been to protect myself, but I felt Ari's hands tighten in my hair, holding my head back.

I figured I'd play dead and just wash it off later, but it turned out to be that Kiss Off® crap that Eva Bloom had been pimping. Something squirmed uncomfortably in my stomach when I thought of her with Mikey.

After more tugging and twisting, Ari managed to sculpt a 'do with a couple of strategically placed braids. I looked at myself in the mirror. Wearing the dress and leggings I'd bought with the whole hair-and-makeup thing, it looked like I was wearing a costume, or a disguise.

"Well, aren't you a pretty little bitch," said a voice muffled by a ski mask. Avery snuck up behind me and wrapped her beefy arms around my shoulders.

"Avery, let go!"

She laughed and released me from her hold. She was wearing this kind of hypervintage 1920s mobster-bitch dress, with rhinestones along the hem. She looked menacing in her jewel-studded ski mask.

"They're not going to let you in with that mask, Ave. Security'll think you're a minor mobster," Kasi said, flirting with herself in the mirror.

Avery shrugged and slipped a cigarette between the mouth-slit of her hand-knited vandal headgear. "Oh, please. Look at me. They'll know I'm major."

"If you're going to smoke, do it out the window," Ari said, raking her fingers through her bangs so they fell even more in her face.

Avery leaned out the window as she lit her cigarette. "You all know that hip-hop gangsta is out and Cosa Nostra is popping now, right?"

"Whatever," Ari said. "On a scale of one to ten—ten being love it, one being hate it—this new style of glorified violence rates an . . . eh."

"An eight?" I asked.

"No. An eh. Total apathy," Ari clarified.

"Oh."

Avery mumbled something vaguely Italian and made like she was going to put out her cigarette on Ari's freshly glittered cheekbone.

Ari took a kickboxing stance and laughed. "Try it, bitch."

Rocket came in then and broke up the fight with a "Ladies, please."

All the Craftsters squealed. Rocket looked stunning. Her dress was simple and stylish, but she was wearing false eyelashes that looked like iridescent butterfly wings that fluttered when she blinked. I stared at them until *my* eyes started to water.

"Hey, I know," Ari said. "Let's see how we rate!"

She started snapping pictures. Rocket opened her eyes wide. Kasi posed playfully against the mirror. Avery knelt on the bed, holding her hands like a pistol aimed at the camera. Tesla brushed the braids out of her face and flipped off the camera irritably. I don't know how my picture looked, I was too surprised to pose.

Ari thrust her intouch® over to me. "Here. Take my picture," she said. She bit her finger seductively, but I laughed because I thought it looked like she was trying to get something out from between her teeth.

"Now time to show the world what luscious bitches we are." She uploaded the pictures somewhere. "I'll send you guys the links to our entries."

Tesla stood up. "Well, they're done. Who wants a heart-throb?"

Tesla's new invention was a kind of high-tech jewelry with diodes inside frosted-ivory beads backed with a conductive plate sensitive to pulse-point electricity. I couldn't follow along with all the technical details, but they were incredible, these heartthrobs. She held one of the moon-colored beads to her wrist and it began blinking to the rhythm of her heartbeat.

"Imagine how great they'll look in low lighting. And after dancing? No doubt we could get those flickers flashing."

She clasped the necklace around her neck, and the little bead jumped to life. Then she went around the room and bejeweled everyone. Avery's light pulsed from an armband buckled to her bare upper arm.

Tesla tied a belt around Kasi's waist, the firefly light winking just below her belly button. She gave Rocket a ring, and slid the headband on Ari, pushing her carmel hair out of her eyes. It looked like she was crowning a queen.

I got the bracelet. It blinked lazily against my wrist.

Ari and Rocket were flipping through the photos on Ari's intouch®, whispering and giggling. I started to get paranoid about what they were saying.

I thought about what Tesla had told me in the car, and the flickering light on my wrist started to speed up.

23 CORPORATIONS THROW THE BEST PARTIES

It was dark when we pulled into the parking lot, but lit like a film set. The whole front of the Game was bright and flashing sponsor names. Halos of blue and yellow colored the air around the building. The darkness kicked back to the edges with flashing red.

Kids huddled in groups out front to share a cigarette or just escape the biomass of the Pit for some autumn night air. The yellowy exterior lighting reflected off the mica flakes in the asphalt, making tiny diamonds on the sidewalk, tiny diamonds in kids' eyes. It made me think of the nature documentaries I'd watched in Cosmonova about nighttime safaris in Africa. Hyenas and pack animals. Everything was glittery and wild. That was my first impression of After Hours.

We stepped up to the glass entryway. The place looked closed, except for the disco-ball fireflies zooming around inside. But we just flashed our IDs and the automatic doors opened with the same wheezy motor whirr like they always did. There was added security at After Hours events. Protecht security guards were checking retinas at the door, looking for the wide-eyed signs of deception and mischief.

"You here to have fun?" a Protecht guard asked me, blinding my right eye with a light.

"Yeah," I mumbled. He paused, not entirely convinced by my reading. He scanned my ID again and must've seen my sponsorship. "Hey, new recruit. You on assignment, then?"

I nodded and he let me pass.

I waited for the other Craftsters. Avery was holding up the line because she kept winking and flirting with the guard.

It took a moment for my eyes to adjust to the dim energy-saving lighting. A purple phantom globe-shadow hung in my vision from the scan. I tried to blink it away.

At the other line, Cayenne Lewis was arguing with a guard who wouldn't let her in. I don't know why, but I walked over to them. "Hey, she's with me," I said, holding up my Game ID again for scanning.

The guard scanned my card.

"Harrison's going to be pleased to know how well those retina scanners are working," I said, name-dropping shamelessly, suddenly worried that I overestimated the amount of

privilege Protecht sponsorship gave me.

The guard just waved us through with a little salute.

I smiled at Cayenne, exhilarated by our little deception.

But she snapped, "Don't think this means I owe you anything."

It was the first time I'd heard her speak and I was surprised at how vulnerable her voice sounded.

"Yeah, whatever. Just stay out of trouble," I said to her back as she disappeared into the crowd.

The Pit glowed an eerie kind of blue-green, and the night sky pushed claustrophobically on the glass ceiling. With metal grates clanked down over the entrances to the rooms and all the other areas closed off, the entire mass of student bodies were crowded into the Pit. The white noise chatter that usually filled this space was all bashed into the shadows by the pulsing music of the Deep Beat DJ from Bangladesh.

For a second I had the feeling that we were all doing something illicit and daring just by being there. Like rave kids throwing parties in warehouses or meatpacking plants in the '90s, or urban explorers finding abandoned malls and hospitals and stuff. But that was totally stupid. The sponsors knew about After Hours—hell, they organized them. They were huge promotional events. Corporations threw the best parties.

Someone grabbed my arm and slapped a wristband around it, cinching it up tight. It was decorated with a black-and-white barcode.

"What's this?" I shouted to Ari.

She was holding up her wrist to get her own band. A girl came along and fastened it to her wrist.

"It's like . . . you scan it and see if you won anything. At the booths."

"Which one?" I asked looking around at all the tables and displays ringing the Pit.

"All of them. You scan them at every booth." I stuck my arm under the crisscrossing red lights of the scanner at the nearest booth. A message flashed up saying, "Sorry. Try again."

Tesla squeezed past me and rushed the dance floor, geeked to test out her new toy and get her heart rate to match the DJ's beats per second.

Ari held on to Rocket's arm and watched the scene. The moon-colored bead flashed steadily against her temple. The light from her heart rate lit up her face, then hid it in blue-green shadows, and again.

"Ooh! Giveaways!" Ari squealed and tugged Rocket's arm. I followed them.

Ari, Rocket, and I went around and crowded into all the booths to scan in. I had no idea what anyone was selling. It was all a blur of excitement and frenzy.

Ari stopped at one of the booths. This one was for like toothpaste. Glow-in-the-dark toothpaste. The promoters at the booth were encouraging kids to brush their teeth with the product and then spit the glowing foam onto a screen, thus creating a canvas of splattered "art." It was pretty gross.

I turned around and saw Ari with a toothbrush in her mouth.

"What're you doing?"

"Wha? 'ts cull."

Luminous drool started to form in the corners of her mouth. She did a shy kind of spit toward the wall, but most of it dribbled down her chin. The crowd applauded anyway and someone handed her a napkin.

"It's cool," Ari said again, wiping her chin. "Look at this." She shoved a brochure in my face so I could read their marketing copy. My eyes glanced over it, not taking a word in.

"It's a really sexy idea." She read the tagline to me: "*When you're ready to fade to black*. And look how white and shiny my smile is." Ari grinned wide and took Rocket's hand again. I thought her teeth looked kind of blue.

"Nice," I said, and looked around. Kids were laughing and talking, their bluish teeth flashing eerily in the dark.

Ari was still smiling. Then she screeched.

"Élan!" She started waving frantically to someone behind me. "Hey!"

A guy came over. He was definitely older, like twenty-three, I guessed. I recognized him from the VIP Lounge. He was catalog-cute: dimples, hair gel, the works. He came over and gave Ari a hug, held on a little too long, but she definitely didn't seem to mind. Her heartthrob was flashing strong; she grinned up at him. She was glowing, literally and figuratively.

"Well, look at you ladies," he said, putting his arm

around her and turning toward us. He did that elevator-eyes thing, scanning our "look" from head to toe. He also had a glow-in-the-dark smile. This guy was so definitely a cool hunter.

"These are my friends," Ari said. "They're branded," she added. "This is Élan," Ari said, leaning her head on his shoulder.

"Hi, Alan," I said, waving.

"It's Élan," he said, kind of annoyed, then he turned the charm back on. "From the old French. It means vigor and liveliness, a distinctive style or flair. Élan."

Ew. I did not like Élan.

He turned back to Ari, tilted her chin up to him. He spoke softly to her, touched her hair. Ari giggled. Then he looked up and saw someone in the crowd. He kissed her forehead and said, "I'll be right back."

Ari spun around. "Can you believe it? Can you believe a brand is flirting with me? How do I look?"

"I believe it," Rocket said. "I always said there had to be some kind of sneaky cheater business happening for you not to be branded already."

"What brand is he scouting for?" I asked.

"He represents Aerwear shoes."

I glanced over in the direction Élan took off to and saw that Ari wasn't the only girl Aerwear shoes was flirting with.

"What's wrong?" Ari said, looking at me.

"I don't know. I feel like . . . I don't know. There's so much going on."

"I know just what you need." Ari told me to stay there and pushed herself through the crowd around the Pedia-fix® booth. I stood there awkwardly with Rocket, listening to the DJ mix Chinese opera, concert piano, and amplified insect noise over shaking bass and deep beat. It was pretty amazing.

"Ari told me that Mikey said that you saw Palmer with Eva in Cosmonova," Rocket said out of nowhere once we were alone. "Why didn't you say anything?"

She stared at me, but I didn't know what to say. Mostly I was surprised that Mikey had been talking about it with Ari.

"I don't know what you heard, but I didn't—"

"You saw them together, right?" she shouted over the music.

"Together, but not, like . . . together. It wasn't any of my business?"

"Well, at least I was betrayed by my enemy and not my *best friend*." She said something else that I couldn't really hear over the music, it sounded like "Jeremy Swift." I scanned the crowd looking for him, but I didn't see what she was talking about.

Ari came back a minute later, grin glowing.

"OK. Close your eyes and hold out your hand."

I did.

She put a little pill in the palm of my hand.

"What's this?" I asked, squinting in the dark at the pill. It said FIX in tiny type.

"It will help you relax and, you know, concentrate. It's good for you."

"Yeah, but what *is* it?"

"It's not dangerous, if that's what you're worried about," Rocket said, irritated. "The administrators agreed it would be safer for the Game if kids had access to better sedatives and stuff."

"I'm cool," I said to Ari, handing the pill back to her.

"Why do you have to be so neg all the time?"

"I'm not neg, I'm just not interested."

Ari rolled her eyes, popped the pill and chased it with some new beverage they were pushing at a nearby booth.

Whatever. Ari and Rocket wanted to walk around the booths some more and scan. I was kind of bored with that scene, but I followed along anyway. I wanted to win something.

Ari picked up necklaces and toys and accessories and cell phone cases and kept saying, "Is this me? Is this me?"

She was like interested in *everything*, but it wasn't with the same enthusiasm as before. I noticed her heartthrob was blinking sort of comatose.

"Is this me?" Ari said again at the next booth.

"Ari. That's, like, a spatula."

Ari turned slowly to look at it. She stared at it, then giggled a little. "Yeah, but should I get it? Is it me?"

"I don't know."

I turned around because there was a lot of commotion at

the table across the way. A kid had won a free game of Buy, Sell & Destroy. A huge plasma screen was showing his game. A crowd surrounded it, watching him play.

Ari stared at the screen, mouth open a little.

"Look at that. It's so grab," she said in a slow monotone. Her eyes were dull but her teeth shone bright.

I watched the kid play, and thought of Jeremy. I thought he wanted to meet me here. I started to get that eely feeling in my stomach again. Maybe he was just playing with me. Maybe he announced to the whole school that he wanted me to come to After Hours just so he could stand me up.

I turned around to share this fear with Ari, but she and Rocket had disappeared. I couldn't see them anywhere.

"You enjoying the music?" a man called out to me. It was Murdoch West from the Hit List. His smile reflected light like normal teeth, but that was the only thing about him that didn't seem artificial. "I've heard so much about you," he said. "Mr. Levy told me you were a talent."

"Yeah?" I said, looking for an escape. I was done talking to cool hunters for the day.

"Yeah." He grinned. "Funny. It never would've come to my attention how many plays your music has been getting from our statistical engines. They're sorted by artist, and you've had quite a number of name changes. . . ."

If he was expecting a charming story about why we kept switching stage names, he wasn't getting it.

"But when we compiled all the tracks you've played on and produced, we found that you and your band rank quite high in on-site playback."

"Oh. Interesting."

"Yes, isn't it? So would you be interested in playing for us sometime?" He gestured to the stage where the DJ was still sweating out beats. "Here at After Hours?"

"What?"

"If we could focus your sound a bit, I'm sure you can be a hit. Of course, we'll have to set up a terms-and-conditions meeting."

"I'm already branded," I said, shrugging. "So. Sorry I can't help you."

He smiled wider. "Oh. Well, I'm sure arrangements can be made—"

"What?" I said cutting him off.

"I said, I'm sure we can—"

"I'm sorry. I can't hear you," I gestured helplessly to the crowd around us.

"Well, maybe we can—"

"Right. It was nice to meet you!" I lied and vanished into the crowd.

I made my way to the edge of the crowd and climbed up the frozen escalator. There were groups of people scattered around the second floor. I snaked around them to get to an empty corner and threw myself down on an out-of-the-way bench.

The track playing now sounded like three balls bouncing on different surfaces and in different rhythms, highlighted with what sounded like a seven-year-old girl sweetly singing a playground rhyme in another language. Bulgarian or Latvian or something.

The music was subjectively good. I mean, I liked it. But I still couldn't make friends with the idea of playing here for Hit List. After dealing with Anica and Harrison, I had the feeling things would be a little more complicated than Murdoch West made it sound.

I wished Mikey wasn't being such a jerk so I could talk to him about this. I looked around for Ari, and hoped she wouldn't get word of Murdoch and his offer.

I stared at the blink blink blink of the heartthrob Tesla gave me. The moon-colored bead on my wrist flashed slowly and rhythmically like a glowing moth beating its wings inside. What was I doing here?

"Hey. I've been looking everywhere for you."

I turned around, surprised to see Jeremy. "Yeah?"

He sat beside me. "Yeah. I was just . . . um. What's that?" He reached down and held my wrist, watched the lazy pulsing of my heartthrob. I tried to explain what Tesla told me, how it worked and stuff. But I forgot all the technical explanations and could only finish with, "It pulses with my heartbeat."

"Really?"

He held my hand a little tighter, staring at the light. All intense. This feeling crept up inside me that he was looking at something private, something he shouldn't be allowed to see.

Just as I thought it, the little light started to blink faster.

Damn, I was being betrayed by my pumping blood-muscle.

Jeremy just sat there beside me calmly watching, or I guess he was calm, how the hell should I know? He didn't have a signal flare brazenly announcing everything he was feeling inside.

Then he was kissing me. Just like that. None of that conscious *Oh, now he's leaning in to kiss me* stuff. Just *Hello, I'm being kissed!*

I started to laugh, a little laugh, but not a giggle. I don't know why. A nervous reaction, maybe? Maybe it was a tickle from his soft lips, or maybe I was just happy.

Whatever the reason for starting, I couldn't stop. I started to worry that he would think something was wrong.

"What?" he said, sounding insecure.

"Nothing," I managed to say, followed by a bubbling laugh, and I kissed him to prove that nothing was wrong.

I couldn't believe I was making out with Jeremy Swift. That out of everyone in the Game, it was me sitting here with his lips pressed to mine.

Then for some effed-up reason, I started thinking about how I was wearing Kiss Off® brand lipstick and the thought echoed in my head, *Is Jeremy man enough to kiss off Kiss Off®? Is Jeremy man enough to kiss off Kiss Off®?*

I started to get a weird feeling, like people were watching me. That this was a kissing contest, and I might not be getting full points. I thought about the "Last Laugh" track. I thought about Mikey. I pulled away, the experience of kissing Jeremy Swift not really feeling how I thought it would.

"Why did you ask me out over intouch®?" I asked. "We were in the VIP Lounge together, why didn't you ask me then?"

"Well, I didn't get a chance to get you alone," he said, putting his arms around me. "You were with Tycho and then Palmer, and then you disappeared."

I kind of wanted to argue with him. He posted on my intouch® stream, where everyone could see because he didn't want to ask me out in front of anybody?

I went to stand by the railing. It was nice to be out of the crowd, up above it. To have a little space. Jeremy stood beside me. I looked up at him, but he was staring at something down in the crowd, frowning.

"How'd she get in?" he said. He was looking at Cayenne Lewis leaning alone against a planter. "I had Harrison put her on the watch list."

"Why her?"

He smiled guiltily and pressed his lips against my temple. "You know," he whispered and wrapped his arms around me. "I saw her carving stuff into Game property. And I know you've been suspicious about her too. It's one of the reasons I mentioned you to my sponsors."

I froze a little. At the Terms and Conditions meeting, Harrison had said Jeremy had "recommended" me. But this sounded more like he had me put on a watch list like Cayenne.

There were squeals and screams from down in the Pit. I could hear them even over the music. About a dozen people wearing white •—• masks were weaving their way through the crowd, throwing water balloons at people dancing. Some people were getting soaked, but they still kept dancing.

Was this an Unidentified prank? I searched the edge of the crowd and saw Cayenne still standing there, arms crossed. Someone launched one of the small blue water balloons out from the crowd and it exploded across her chest. She was not amused.

24 APOLOGIES

I couldn't find Ari or any of the Craftsters down in the crowd. I checked my intouch®.

kidzero: can't find you on the dance floor. time to go?

I hung around the edge of the crowd, watching people. Not recognizing anyone. Waiting. I held my intouch® lifeless in my hand.

I went out to wait by Tesla's car, but it wasn't in the parking lot. There were no messages from Ari or the others saying they were going to leave or anything, but they had left. I'd told Mom I was going to stay at Ari's, but I guess plans had changed. I wasn't in the mood for the Truth-or-Dares of the Craftsters anyway, but it was still really shitty of them to leave me without a ride home.

kidzero: nice. how am i supposed to get home?

I didn't really expect an answer, and was kind of upset with myself for broadcasting how much they'd gotten to me. Tesla replied a few minutes later though.

toy321: ??? ari said youre getting a ride home with swift. @KID

toy321: sorry. @KID

Jeremy had left already, and there definitely hadn't been any talk about him taking me home. Mom would freak the eff out. Though I wonder how her maternal brain would weigh the cost-benefit ratios of a ride home with a boy vs. no ride home at all.

Because I didn't have a ride home.

I stood outside the front of the Game, my hoodie a little too thin to keep me warm and the night breeze blowing up my skirt in spite of the leggings. The huge parking lot was slowly emptying of all its cars. The red taillights snaked off into the darkness. A car passed by with Abercrombie Fletcher hanging out of the passenger window, howling at the night.

I leaned against a low wall and pretended that I was also waiting for a ride. Who was I trying to fool? Maybe myself. I couldn't stand admitting that the girls who I thought were my friends would abandon me so completely. And for what?

I pushed away from the wall and started walking.

A car pulled up beside me.

"Do you need a ride?"

I bent down to see who was driving. It was Cayenne. I kind of laughed, but nothing about this night was very funny.

"Just let me take you where you want to go," she said impatiently. "I don't like being in debt."

I got into the car, pulled the door shut behind me. I mumbled directions to where I lived and didn't say anything else.

Cayenne just drove on in silence.

I peeked over at her. When we passed under streetlights her face lit up white, and I could see the metal studs lining her ear, her pink cheek tattoo, and the cute curve of her nose. Her clothes were wet from the water balloon attack. Stained blue, by the look of it.

She kept her eyes focused on the road. I wanted to ask her why the Unidentified had soaked her or thank her for saving my ass and giving me a ride home. But I wasn't going to risk polluting the silence. I could keep quiet. I turned to look out the window.

"Your friends ditch you?" she asked out of nowhere.

"No," I lied. "Did yours?"

She kind of laughed. "Nah, they didn't have an escort

through security like some people. I'm sure your sponsors will be delighted that their control is impenetrable."

"But the water balloons . . . ?"

"That wasn't us," she snapped.

She flicked a piece of blue water balloon at me and I saw the words BLUE RUIN® printed on it.

"Apparently, it's a really cool new drink," she said, fake-chipper. "Pure water dyed cleaning-fluid blue."

She stared angrily at the road.

"What's your boss going to say?" My heartthrob started to flash annoyingly when I mentioned him, and I pulled my sweatshirt sleeve over my wrist to hide it.

"He's not our boss," she snorted.

"Who is he?"

She leaned over and started yelling into my hoodie pocket as if I were recording our conversation on my intouch®. "Yeah, right, Protecht. I'm not naming names."

"I wasn't . . . I wouldn't," I stuttered defensively, but I thought of Jeremy and how confusing his connection to Protecht made things, and decided I wouldn't trust myself either. "Besides, I would be more worried about Trend-setters."

I noticed Cayenne get tense, sit a little straighter. "Oh, yeah?"

"Anica was asking about you. Well, not you personally. But the Unidentified." I couldn't stop. "Well, okay. Maybe she mentioned you, too."

"What did she say?"

205

"Something about Palmer being a heartbreaker?"

"Not about that!" she almost shouted. "I meant, what did she say about the Unidentified?"

"She said Trendsetters were trying a new strategy. That they wanted to be *relevant* to a different crowd. That being a rebel never goes out of style."

"Sounds like something she'd say," Cayenne muttered.

"Look, I didn't know they were branding me to somehow get to you guys. I didn't know."

"Get used to getting used," she said quietly.

"That's me there," I said, pointing to my driveway. All the lights were off at home.

Cayenne turned into the driveway and let the car idle.

"Just . . ." she began. "It's not easy to know who your friends are. So don't take it personally."

"Don't take what personally?"

"When I go back to pretending you don't exist."

I laughed because I thought she was joking, but she sat there gripping the steering wheel, staring out the windshield, waiting for me to leave.

"Right," I said, getting out of the car and slamming the door.

The car stood there humming quietly, like it wanted to say more, but wasn't going to.

I climbed the steps to the front door before I remembered that the cardkey to my house was tied to my orange shoelace, tied to the belt loop of the pants that lay crumpled in a pile in Ari's bedroom. I just hoped Mom wouldn't get pissed at me for waking her up so late.

I rang the bell. I rang it a couple times.

The lights didn't go on, but I heard the keypad tones and locks slide out of place. Mom opened the door.

"What're you doing home? I thought you were staying at Ari's," she said when she saw me. "Who's that?" She watched Cayenne's unfamiliar car pull out of the driveway.

"A friend from school," I muttered. "I didn't feel like staying out," I lied. "And she offered to bring me home."

Mom looked at me, apparently unprepared to come up with a lecture on the dangers of coming home. I kissed her good night and hurried to my room before she could ask me about my night.

I checked my intouch® just to see if Ari apologized or something for ditching me.

The last message from her was the link for the *Rate It!* site. I went to it.

There was the picture Ari took of me in my new clothes looking startled and uncomfortable.

According to votes, it said I was a 2.5. Halfway between *You're a Skeezy Crack Whore* and *You Are One of the Unwashed Masses*.

Most of the Craftsters got sixes—*Yeah, You're Pretty Cute*—except Avery, who got an eight, *You Are a Classic Pinup Girl*.

Some of the anonymous comments on my picture were vicious. I couldn't stop reading and rereading them. I didn't understand why people would say things like that about me when they didn't even know me. Then I finally closed it down.

There was a message on my Network page.

Apologies. *by mikes*

Mikey never said the words "I'm sorry." I stared at the message, thinking about what Cayenne had said. *Sometimes it's hard to know who your friends are.* But sometimes it was really easy.

In the glow of my Network page, I sent a private message to Mikey.

Are you sleeping? Say no. *by kidzero.*

I never sleep. *by mikes.*

I laughed. I'd seen Mikey fall asleep in the most uncomfortable places—hunched over a desk in Math Attack, sprawled out on a bus stop bench, cuddled up beside Lump—but he would always maintain that he never slept.

My fingers hovered over the keyboard. So many times tonight I wished I could talk to Mikey, and now that I had him here I didn't know what to say.

I was kind of afraid. Afraid of what he could say.

Say something. *by kidzero.*

Like what? *by mikes.*

Like that we're ok? *by kidzero.*

We're ok, *by mikes.*

I stared at his words for a while, trying to feel if they were true. It felt true. He sent another note.

I'd ask how things went tonight. But I really really really don't want to know. *by mikes.*

After Hours. Bleh. *by kidzero.*

But how was the music? *by mikes.*

The music was win win win win win. But I got ambushed by the Hit List guy. They tracked us down. *by kidzero.*

What did he want? *by mikes.*

He wanted to know if we wanted to play at After Hours. *by kidzero.*

Really? And do we want to? *by mikes.*

I thought about it. What did I really want?

I wouldn't mind playing. But I'm not that excited about doing it at After Hours. Or for Hit List. *by kidzero.*

What did Ari say? *by mikes.*

I didn't want to admit that she ditched me. Even to Mikey. Maybe especially to Mikey.

Hey, when did you tell Ari about what happened in Cosmonova? Rocket asked me about it? *by kidzero.*

Awkward. And I didn't tell her. Ari started blabbing about what a big drama it was. Like OMG! DID YOU HEAR? PALMERROCKETEVA. OMG! And I told her I already knew. That we were unfortunate enough to witness the disheveled aftermath of the unholy union firsthand. *by mikes.*

Yeah, well. Like you said. AWKWARD. And speaking of unholy unions . . . Eva Bloom? Why?

But I deleted it before I sent. Delete, delete, delete. I wanted to know, but I never wanted to know.

I sent: Yeah, well. Like you said. AWKWARD. *by kidzero.*

I told him about all the DJ sounds at After Hours, joked with him about stupid details to cover up the painful truths. I didn't mention Jeremy. Didn't tell him about Cayenne.

You coming to the War Game on Sunday? I'm cheering for the Princesses. 150%. *by mikes.*

I thought Swift was your boy. *by kidzero.*

I thought he was yours. *by mikes.*

Whatever. Save the Princess 4ever! *by kidzero.*

YEAH! Swift can take a virtual sniper bullet to the groin. *by mikes.*

Wow. That was . . . um, graphic. *by kidzero.*

We spent the next forever writing back and forth. He made me forget the hollow hurt of being left. Helped me untangle the complicated everything that had been overwhelming me since I got branded. He wasn't here, but he felt close.

25 COORDINATES

I got up way late the next day. In the living room I noticed
a Trendsetters delivery box that must've come for me when
I had been getting ready at Ari's. I opened it to find some
clothes and a note from Anica.

I think you'll enjoy our new look.

A Lass

The box was filled with I AM A TARGET MARKET T-shirts.
A skirt silk-screened with the Unidentified •–• face, and a
dress with an intricate question mark pattern. The worst
thing about the package was that I *would* wear these clothes.
If I didn't know the cynical backstory to these products, I
would buy them.

I went to the kitchen to get breakfast, leaving the box

like a guilty conscience. While I ate, Mom ran through a droning monologue about being where I told her I'd be, punctuated with high-pitched *Are you listening to me?*s.

"And keep your intouch® on at all times," she added.

"You told me to keep it off after closing time because of roaming fees."

"Don't tell me what I told you to do!" she shouted, completely unreasonable now.

I stood up and flipped on my intouch®. "There!" I shouted. "Now you can see that I'll be in my room."

"Go to your room!" she shouted back, a little too late.

I slammed my door and locked it. I tossed myself onto my bed and opened my notebook®. I scrolled through the chat I had with Mikey last night, thankful again that our conversation was password-protected. While I was in the middle of composing a passionate critique of all my mother's failures as a logical being, I got a new message.

39.954276N 75.165651W
15:30
•—•

by anonymous

I clicked over to the mapping software to check the coordinates. It was a park in the city center.

I wish I could say I hesitated. That I remembered all the Protecht security tips. That I thought over all the pros and cons of sneaking out right now to meet some people who I knew had less-than-legal extracurricular activities. But I didn't.

I punched the coordinates to my room into my notebook® and synched my intouch® to the mapping software, trusting Elle's Alibi to keep my secrets safe.

Mom would be leaving for Aunt Gillie's soon. I turned my music on, checked the door again. I'd spent so many countless hours alone in my room listening to music nonstop that this was the easy part of my alibi. From the speakers, the fly buzzed against the glass in my *Background Checks* song.

I opened the window.

Mom didn't think it was safe for me to ride my bike, but it was the only way I could get into the city. She forced me to do it. If she had been reasonable and authorized my Game card to be accepted on the metro, I wouldn't have to take drastic actions to get out of the house.

But my intouch® was keeping my secrets. I was moving fast and no one knew my trajectory. This was probably what Mikey meant when he talked about "breeze." I always thought he was referring to simple speed, but there was probably this feeling of freedom in his word choice.

I rode to the city, enjoying the breeze.

It wasn't until I got closer to the park that I started to feel the doubt about what I was doing. I mean, this was my mother's worst nightmare *exactly*.

When I got to the coordinates, I bent over to lock my bike. Someone leapfrogged over the bike rack and landed close beside me. I stumbled backward, scared.

"Not regretting meeting up with a stranger from the interweb, are you?" he said, grinning. "Come on."

He was wearing the Urban Climber harness over his dark anti-scenester clothes. He turned and took the steps two at a time, hustling up a low dividing wall.

I couldn't believe I was following him.

He hopped down from the four-foot ledge in a move both skillful and reckless. "Cayenne said you helped her through security last night."

I slid down after him, resting my foot on the back of a park bench and stepping down carefully.

"I guess," I answered.

"Why?"

I shrugged. I didn't have a good answer, or any answer. "There was a scene at After Hours. They made it look like an Unidentified stunt."

"Yeah, I heard." He took a seat on the bench. "Well, next time we have to make sure there'll be no mistake," he said, squinting up at me.

I sat down beside him, my fingers played with a •–• carved into the bench. "What does this mean?"

"It's the symbol of our disinterest in what they're telling us. That we are not impressed."

"Yeah, well, what's it going to mean when they start using it to sell stuff to people who are disinterested and generally unimpressed?"

"This is a movement," he said. "It's something real."

I was getting kind of nervous again. "Where's everyone

else? Cayenne and Tycho and the others."

He laughed. "Sophia told me you used the Network's friends list to track them down. It's an inherent flaw in their system. They use your connections to trap you in a social web. But there are ways to get free of their control."

He smiled, but I was still uncomfortable. I looked around. "Aren't they coming?" I asked again.

"No, but we're going to meet them." He grinned. "You don't want to get caught loitering here, do you?"

He was right. We couldn't sit here in this public space for long without getting hassled by the authorities.

"Come on."

"I shouldn't."

"Why? You're not afraid of *me*, are you?"

"I don't even know who you are." I stood up. I was feeling something that was probably fear if I could admit that. "Who are you?"

He got to his feet too. "How am I supposed to answer that? You want a name? You want to know my likes and dislikes? To list the ethnicity of my ancestors? Would knowing any of these things answer your question? There aren't answers to all questions. The simplest questions are the hardest ones." He leaned in close. "Who are *you*?"

I opened my mouth to answer, but nothing came.

"Who are you when you're alone? When no one is watching? What's left then?"

My mind was empty. I couldn't think of a single thing that felt true.

I watched his lips as he spoke.

"You are the unidentified."

The door slid shut with the finality of my decision. I was going with him. I was sitting *in the van* of a strange guy who just answered "Can't" when I asked him why he couldn't tell me his name.

He had loaded my bike into the back, then climbed into the driver's seat. When he held up his card to authorize the ignition, I was already starting to regret this. The motor cleared its throat, then continued to run silently.

The van slowly pulled away from the curb.

It hadn't even taken much to get me to go with him. Just a promise. He told me there was a place the Unidentified met. A place where they could sit for hours without the authorities harassing them. A place where intouch® signals were blocked. A place where they could talk without being overheard.

He promised freedom.

Things you are told are freedoms in fact limit your choices.

That was true. There were only two choices. Go or don't go. I went.

But maybe I was choosing my suicide?

I laughed.

"What?" he asked.

"Nothing," I said, and returned to the uncomfortable outer-spacey silence. I watched the street signs and the people on the sidewalks and felt the separation between them and me. In the passenger seat of a stranger's van, no one can hear you scream. I laughed again, my nervous reaction.

"You OK?" he said.

"Maybe I should just—"

"We're here."

We hadn't gone very far. Just a few blocks through the city. Five minutes of regret.

"Here?"

We'd stopped in front of a prison. An ancient prison, unused for decades, but still standing in the center of the city.

I jumped down to the curb, relieved to be out of the van, but not exactly excited about the prospect of breaking into a prison. "How are we supposed to get in?"

He waved me over to the intersection, away from the wall. "This connects to one of the incomplete inmate escape tunnels." He stood there holding open the grate to a storm drain, right in the middle of the sidewalk. Carefree in the bright afternoon sunlight.

"How did you find this?"

"Let's just say I'm good at finding weaknesses in people's defenses." He reached out his hand to me. "After you."

The choices were always the same. Do it, or don't.

He lowered the grate behind the both of us. Grinning in the damp underground.

He whispered stories about famous escapes as we stepped carefully, crouched underground. "The prisoners we remember are the ones who escaped."

"Yeah, but those stories were about the ones who got caught trying to escape. Not the ones who got away."

"Huh, OK. You win."

The tunnel led up to a cell block. All the barred doors stood open, rusty at their hinges. The sunlight highlighted the clouds of dust from our footsteps and increased the contrast of the cracks in the stone.

"So this place is just abandoned?" I asked, looking up at the individual skylights. "No one comes here?"

"We come here," he said, leading me through the long corridors. "The stone walls block intouch® tracking signals, and it's fitting, don't you think?"

"I don't . . . How?"

"The abandoned shopping centers were reappropriated for use as the education institutions of the Game, and we're reappropriating the penitentiary into the headquarters of our resistance." He ran his hand across the wall and pieces of it flaked off and rained to the floor. "They should've used prisons, right? When they were proposing the Game? If they were going to take over existing architecture, what better way?"

"The Game isn't a prison," I argued, weaving around the rubble of a crumbled wall. "It's the only place we get to actually *do* anything, where we're allowed to be."

"It's a system that makes the inmates grateful for their lockdown." He leaned his weight to push open a door. "Hah. You lose."

"Do you always keep score?"

He turned and stepped closer to me, leaned down, and whispered, "Always."

I followed him out into the yard. "Observation tower," he said, pointing to the dominating structure in the center. "Isolation cells. Warden's office." He took the stairs two at a time in the administration building. "The Game keeps us isolated from the outside world. How is that *not* a prison?"

He opened the door to a small office where I was met with semi-hostile stares from each of the Unidentified.

"What's she doing here?" Sophia asked.

"I thought we were planning a party, and everyone's invited?" he replied, joining the group.

Cayenne looked away and focused on her notebook® screen again, not saying a word. Tycho and Lexie kind of watched me from the sofa. I stood there awkwardly. They were the Unidentified, and I was the uninvited. What was I doing here?

Elijah whispered something to Sophia then came over to greet me.

"How's Mikey?" Elijah asked.

"OK, I guess."

"Tell him I said hi."

"Yeah, OK." I waited three forever-seconds, then added, "So, you're planning a party?"

"We are indeed," the voice of the Unidentified announced. He was perched in front of a window overlooking the prison yard.

I felt the intensity of Cayenne's irritation from across the room.

"It's going to be epidemic," he continued. "An event to announce to the administrators that they can't stop the force of our dissatisfaction. Once the word gets out."

"A protest party?" I interrupted. "But haven't you seen the news? Those don't do anything."

Lexie rolled her eyes and muttered something to Tycho. Way to make friends and influence people, Kid.

"Maybe," he said, jumping down from the windowsill. "But maybe an invitation to protest is more powerful than the protest itself."

"She doesn't need to know everything," Cayenne snapped, still not looking at me.

"Not everyone can keep a secret like you can, Cayenne." He grinned at her, then turned back to me. "What if the meaning wasn't in the message? What if it was only a way to deliver a deeper idea? A method of distribution."

I had no idea what he was talking about.

"What are you doing?" Tycho spoke up. "Don't you know who her sponsors are?"

"A pariah virus," he whispered, so close to me now.

I saw Lexie and Sophia exchange frowns.

"It's a nasty little virus that infects only the Network system. It publishes all the user's password-protected secrets to everyone in their contact list." He slipped his arm around me. "The only way to stop it is to delete all your contacts before the attack phase. Can you imagine a system-wide status change? Everyone, all of us, dropping out of the system? The solidarity of choosing to be united by nothing?"

Cayenne stood up and shoved past him to leave the room. He watched her go.

"I hope you know what you're doing," Tycho muttered.

"What's she going to do? Tell her sponsors?" He smiled at me. "I know who I can trust."

26 WAR GAMES

Out in front of the Game entrance the next day, I confided in Mikey about my prison break-in.

He basically freaked out.

"Are you *insane?*" he shouted. "You could've . . . You could've . . . Do you even know what could've happened?"

"Yeah, sorry, Mom. I didn't mean to offend your sensitive sensibilities. Elijah said hi, by the way."

"What?"

I just shrugged. "Besides, it's not like *you* never do anything reckless."

Mikey had a legitimate police record. He had "borrowed" his dad's car one night after he got his license. No easy feat, since he had to hack the authorization lockout.

But he got it running, hilarity ensued, until his dad called the cops on him.

It was a completely disproportionate punishment for taking the car without asking. I mean, it wasn't like Mikey pistol-whipped his dad and stole his ride. But because Mikey tricked the technology, the judge wanted to make it a big kids-don't-try-this-at-home case and suspended his license and restricted his public access to a single home-to-Game route until he came of age.

"That's not the same," Mikey said, frowning. "What did he want, anyway?"

"He wanted to . . ." I decided not to tell Mikey about the virus, but I wasn't really sure why. I think I wanted to prove to the Unidentified that I could keep their secrets. "He wanted to introduce me to the rest of the group." Was that why he took me there? He wanted me involved in their future plans anyway. Somehow.

"Oh my Google, it's a cult!" he wrapped his arms around me like he was shielding me from a bomb blast. "I won't let them brainwash you!"

I laughed. "You want to go in? Get decent seats?"

"OK," he said, but still not releasing me.

"Mikey!" I shouted, and he let me go, laughing.

Inside, things were already revving up for the big War Game. The maintenance crews had synced the screens in the Pit into a single huge screen where the video battle would play. The elaborate stage where the two teams would be seated in front of their own monitors had already been set up. One of the workers was still untangling the console cords.

"But seriously," Mikey said, taking a seat beside me. "Who was that guy? You're not seriously considering getting involved with them, are you?"

"I don't know."

"Don't," he said, popping a handful of Javajacks into his mouth. "It's so trendy already." He gestured around to some people in the crowd. They were wearing I AM A TARGET MARKET T-shirts.

That was fast.

"Hey, have you heard from Ari?" I said, checking my intouch®. "She disappeared at After Hours and I haven't heard from her."

"Maybe she ran off to join the Unidentified."

I shoved him, and turned my attention to the people around us.

The crowd was so hyped for the game, crackling with energy. TV crews from the sports stations were there covering the public event. It was open entrance for families and friends so they could come out in costume to support their team. The Pit was filled with screaming fans waving team colors: burgundy and black for Meat Hammer, silver and white for the Princesses. Mikey stood beside me, hooting and booing alternately.

p_phillips: can you even see anything from down there? @KID

Scanning the scene, I saw Palmer Phillips sitting in the VIP box seats with the other people on the It List. He waved.

I waved awkwardly back, not really understanding why he would be buzzing me.

p_phillips: swift asked me to save you a seat @KID

p_phillips: your boy wanted to make sure you had a good view of him blasting face @KID

I quickly thumbed back.

kidzero: i'm watching the game with friends, thanks. @PALMER

I put my intouch® away and pretended not to notice Mikey checking my stream on his own intouch®. I wished all my friends didn't know *every time* someone shouted me out on my stream.

Luckily, the speakers blared the title music, so if Mikey felt the need to make a joke about my new buddy Palmer, I wouldn't be able to hear it now over the music and the ocean roar of the crowd.

The giant screen up front started to flash video stats of each of the players before they took the stage. We could see their season scores, weapon of choice, and which brand was sponsoring their play lit up large for all to see.

Meat Hammer's team captain, screen-name kill0ne,

came out first in full slacker-warrior gear. He took the stage, fists pumping in the air, as the crowd cheered and jeered. His oversized portrait on the screen glowered out at the crowd.

Jeremy came out after him. His screen-name, swiftx, flashed below his picture on the screen, making it look like a mug shot. The way his dark hair fell over his squinty eyes made him look like a criminal superstar.

Junkmonkey took the stage next, jumping up and down and waving his arms wildly at the crowd. But the picture behind him was of Aggro8, who came onstage to pull Junkmonkey off again. The crowd laughed, but Aggro8 saluted solemnly and took a seat.

Then up on the screen, we saw Junkmonkey's out-of-focus photo—as if he had moved when the picture was taken. We all laughed and craned our necks, searching the empty stage for some sign of him, but he was still backstage. Then he came running out and attempted to do a cartwheel. He failed spectacularly and the crowd cheered.

Kill0ne and Aggro8 were watching Junkmonkey's antics disapprovingly, but Jeremy wasn't even paying attention; he scanned the crowd.

When Save the Princess took the stage, I got swept up in the energy and squealed like a fangirl. In each of their pictures, they looked straight at the camera, expressionless and in control.

Elle (screen-name Elle) came out first. She was wearing an all-white track suit. Her hair glowed silver in the stage lighting, her eyes shaded by her pink-tinted glasses. She stood on the side of the stage, waiting for the rest of her players.

Kasi Mohindra (screen-name Mo) followed after Elle. She looked tiny on the big stage. Kasi had embroidered the number of kills she got over the season onto the sleeve of her uniform. Her entire arm was polka-dotted with multi-colored skulls that continued onto her back. She pushed a strand of dark hair behind her ear and waved to the crowd before walking over to stand next to Elle.

Tesla (toy321) came out next, wearing simple fatigues and her flipstream goggles. They made her eyes bulge like fishbowls, and when she blinked, her lower lashes rose to the top. She looked surreally lizard-like.

"Oh shit! She's going to play the game *flipped*." Mikey laughed. "This is psychological warfare at its finest."

Tesla was showing the meatpounders that she was so confident in her skill, she could play the game upside-down. But I was worried about what the administrators would do with her flaunting their ban like that. She turned to the seated Meat Hammer players and flashed them a peace sign, then stood beside Mo.

Lexie Phillips, AKA Widow9, took the stage last. Her fatigues were embellished with tiny personalized details: zombie-bunny good-luck charms, barbed-wire bracelets. It was rare that a newbie got a spot on a League team. I wondered if the Unidentified came out to support her game today.

After all four of the Princesses were lined up together onstage, they turned at the same time and marched to their seats in front of their monitors, solemnly and professionally. They looked crazy intimidating.

In every War Game, the two teams face off against each other in three rounds, in accordance with the Major League Gaming rules. First up was Capture the Flag, where the teams had to quickly control the map, yank the flag from the other team's base, and run it back to their own without getting tagged in the back by a grenade or plasma blast. First team to successfully capture the flag three times won that round.

The title screen started up, and the crowd stomped their feet, charging up for the round to start. I could hardly hear the starting buzzer over the shouting and laughter. I squeezed Mikey's hand, and watched as all eight players spawned on screen, their avatars materializing out of nothingness onto the battlefield.

All the players were miked up so the crowd could hear the strategies and team planning, but the crowd could hear everything else too. Trash talk was booming out through the Pit.

"You're substandard, Kill-one! Why do you even play this game?" Mo taunted.

"Yeah, yeah. Snipe a guy when he spawns. That's so cheap!" Junkmonkey was having a hard time getting into the game, Widow9 kept picking him off before he could take a step forward.

Save the Princess was way competent at Capture the Flag, because they were so focused and worked together so tight. Elle grabbed the flag, tossed it up on base where toy321 was waiting. She grabbed it while Mo laid down fire in front of her.

"Ooh! Plasma blast to the face. Did that hurt, meat-pounder?" Elle, of course.

Toy321 got picked off as soon as she entered home base, but Widow9 was there to grab the fallen flag before the boys could get their hands on it. Lexie was definitely a skill player.

1-0, Save the Princess. The spectators shouted their support, and I felt my throat go raw with my screams even though I couldn't hear myself.

Meat Hammer was crude, but the Princesses were raunchy. They skillfully wielded a brand of shit talk that made these hyper-testosteroned meatgeeks blush. The boys practically dropped their controllers, and the Princesses cleaned up easy in the first round, 3-1.

The crowd erupted at the Princesses' win. I jumped up and hugged Mikey. He hugged me back hard.

"I thought you were still secretly backing Meat Hammer!" I shouted into Mikey's ear.

Mikey mumbled something I couldn't hear over the noise, even though his mouth was right by my ear.

We let go of each other. Mikey looked at me for a second, then turned back to the screen. The Team Slayer round was starting. The first team to reach fifty kills won the round, and Meat Hammer had taken an early lead.

Both teams were getting hit hard, but it was still pretty even since one of the Meats—Aggro8, I think—even though he racked up a string of kills, obviously didn't value his own life enough to play smart and use cover. The Princesses were always just two kills behind, they could still cinch it.

The energy in the crowd was mad now, and then I heard something that sounded like firecrackers up on the second floor. I mean, there was a lot of booming and blasting coming from the surround speakers, but these pops and cracks sounded raw.

Then someone started the crowd chanting. I couldn't hear what everyone was saying right away, but it was spreading into a chorus. The firecracker pops were still going off, and then a bottle rocket with tail blazing streaked over the stage. I held on to Mikey's hand and gasped along with everyone else. Some of the players up on stage even took their eyes off the screen as it whizzed in the air over the crowd.

The air filled with that kind of firework smell. A tangy gunpowder scent that stung my nose. The crowd was still laughing and chanting, but I started to feel that something was wrong.

Mikey and I stood up on our chairs and looked around. Weaving their way through the mob, I saw a few people wearing flesh-colored but faceless plastic masks. They were wrapped in bloody bandages, showing gruesome war wounds.

Then doll parts rained down from the second floor. Soaked in red paint.

"It's them!" I shouted into Mikey's ear, gripping his arm tight now.

It had to be them. The Unidentified. The fake blood, the violent shock. This wasn't a sponsored scene. It was the real thing.

The voices of the crowd grew more and more rhythmic until words formed from the rumble. I heard the crowd's gleeful chant, "War! UGH! What is it good for?" but instead of the "absolutely nothing" part, people were squealing, "killing lots of bodies." Huh, good God.

Hardly anyone was paying attention to the War Game now, the crowd was worked up into a bizarre frenzy by all of the smoke and firecrackers and mutilated doll parts getting tossed around. People were starting to shove. The crowd lurched back into me and I was knocked off my chair, hard.

Mikey called out, "Kid!"

I fell and landed painfully on the tile floor. Hip, shoulder, head. The three spots on my body throbbed in order of contact on the hard floor. I put my hands up to protect my head, to keep people from stepping on it. Some kids who saw me fall tried to help me up, but other people had no clue I was down there and kept trampling me.

I looked up and saw Mikey jump down from his chair, pushing people away to get to me.

Someone's hands gripped my sore shoulders and helped me to my feet. I turned around, my mouth open to thank him. But I found one of those faceless masks looking back at me, and I lost all words. The human eyes peeking out from behind that eerily inhuman face looked so creepy-wrong.

Mikey pushed his way past the spectators, and stepped up in between the masked guy and me. Mikey grabbed the guy's wrist to break the grip on my arm. "Leave her alone," he said, and pushed him back, a two-hands-to-the-chest shove.

As the masked man stumbled backward a few steps, the hood of his sweatshirt fell back and I saw the dreadlocks. The iconic mullet of the Unidentified leader.

Mikey turned to ask me if I was okay, and I saw the mask face loom up behind him with a smile in his eyes that didn't match the expressionless plastic face. Then the guy, the mask-man, punched Mikey in the back of the head.

Mikey fell forward against the chairs, then got to his knees.

I yelled into the face that wasn't a face, "Why are you doing this?" and turned to help Mikey.

I saw how angry Mikey was, and I was worried about what he was going to do next.

Mikey turned to look at me. "Who—?"

But the mask-man appeared out of nowhere again and pushed Mikey hard into the people in front of him. Like a reaction of a wave, the crowd shoved back and Mikey smashed into mask-man again.

This time Mikey was ready. The mask took a swing, but Mikey ducked it. Then they started to brawl, like a rolling-on-the-floor, fists-flying-everywhere fight. The crowd, like a conscious entity, started to reshape itself to make room for them. More people were watching their fight than what was happening on-screen, I couldn't imagine *anyone* was still watching what was happening on-screen.

I just heard myself yelling, "Mikey!" over and over again, but at the same time, I couldn't hear anything. It was like being underwater, or watching a film with frame-skips. I could not make sense of what was happening. Mikey was on the ground, struggling to free himself, but that guy was just hitting him. Why wasn't anyone doing anything?

Mikey was flopping and flailing and managed to throw up an elbow into the guy's face. There was a sickening crack. The nose was hard plastic, impossible to break, but the nose under it wasn't. Blood seeped out from under the mask.

Mikey stumbled over some chairs trying to get his balance, not really aware of how much damage he'd done.

Protecht mall security in their pork-colored polyester jackets and toy-looking walkie-talkies finally cut through the crowd. Security supervisor Harrison grabbed Mikey, and another guard lunged to get a hold of the guy behind the mask. But he had retreated back into the now-riotous crowd. He was gone.

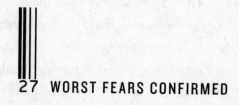

27 WORST FEARS CONFIRMED

On the news that night, our Game site administrators were on the TV saying that it was "regrettable" that when the Game was opened to the public, the problems of the outside world found their way inside. They were using this tragedy to lock down the Game even more, institute tighter security procedures.

Mrs. Bond gave her sound bite up on-screen: "The only thing controversial about our business model is that we give children power, the power of consumers. Their choices and interests dictate what we provide. Education is tailored to give the student, the consumer, what he or she wants. The people responsible for this attack *want* to disrupt our way of life. As site administrators, we won't allow it."

In the background, firework smoke made the air hazy and little groups of the mob felt free to continue on with some residual vandalism. Kids were jumping off chairs, pushing each other around. Parents held players' younger siblings in their arms, trying to make their way to the exit.

They didn't say anything about Mikey, and that was the only news I cared about. Instead, they spent time debating what the score had been before the disruption, and how the matter of championship scoring should be settled.

No mention of the Unidentified at all. They were able to name-drop a bunch of sponsors, however, getting them free publicity from the coverage. Mrs. Bond even managed to plug After Hours by assuring parents that Protecht security had proven successful at the Friday night events and would continue to be a wholesome socializing experience for the youth of the community.

"I don't want you going to any more public access events," Mom said. She got such a perverse pleasure from bad news, she probably liked to see her worldview confirmed. My intouch® had been eerily still all night. Jeremy and Tesla had given some updates. Tesla's confirmed what the championship rules said about contingency scoring, and Jeremy fired off:

swiftx: the people who effed up the war game . . .

swiftx: . . . they'll pay for that free-for-all.

But I didn't care about any of that. I held my intouch®, hoping to see something from Mikey. I wanted proof that he didn't have to give back his intouch®, that he was still in the Game.

28 SELLING REBELLION

Mikey wasn't in the Game the next day. His Network page was down and I didn't know how to get in contact with him. He didn't answer any of my intouch® texts, and I was starting to worry that he wasn't getting them.

I stared at my unresponsive intouch® and tried to think of how I could find out if Mikey was okay. Maybe Winterson would know?

Palmer intercepted me as I was crossing the Pit.

"Hey! Where're you going? We're all meeting in the lounge."

"Oh. I don't—"

"You have to come! You were in the middle of it. Did you know that was going to happen? How often does a spotter get a break like that? You have inside tips, right?"

"What are you talking about?"

"The War Game Riot!"

He steered me over to the VIP Lounge. The It Listers were gathered in small groups chatting animatedly. I saw Tycho Williams standing to the side, trying to avoid my eyes.

"Hey," I said, jaw tensed in an unconvincing smile. "I didn't see you at the War Game."

He glanced up at me. "Yeah. I . . . I had to take care of my little sister."

"Oh. Nice alibi."

He started to say something, but was interrupted by Palmer Phillips addressing the room. "OK, then. Let's get to today's top story. This one is a real rumor riot so we need to do what we're best at and tame the trend, control the flow, and sensibly sensationalize. You all have your fingers to the pulse, so you know I'm talking about the disturbance during the War Game yesterday." He grinned and his fang-tooth sparkled.

He continued, "You know the sponsors' stance on violence: fun for the whole family until someone loses an eye. So, let's hear it, what did all you trendsetters think?"

"You know, I think it was kind of beautiful?" Echo Petersson spoke up with her kind of breathy high-pitched voice. "How the whole crowd started chanting as one?"

"Yeah, it seemed so natural," Abe Fletcher added. "And easy, like you could get the crowd to say anything, because we were together and, like, a part of something. It was better

239

than viral, it was, um . . . "

"Emergent?" Palmer suggested.

A lot of people muttered excitedly.

"Yeah, and I just wanted to say?" Verity Clark spoke up, her voice rising at the end, punctuating everything she said like a question. "You don't really get to see blood very much in real life, right? I mean, it's in the movies and on TV everywhere? But there's something really POWERFUL with real blood," she added almost reverently. "Is there a way we can use blood more in campaigns? I mean, tastefully, like for Band-Aids, maybe?"

I squirmed uncomfortably at the thought of the spokesgirl for Time of Your Life teen tampons suggesting more blood in advertising. But blood sounded good to these lopsided vampires. It was weird to sit in on a focus group for a protest.

I nudged Tycho. "I bet you didn't know the Unidentified would be so popular with this crowd. I'm sure your leader will find it satisfying to know he's got so many fans," I hissed. "Is that why he did it? For attention?"

Tycho shushed me. "Not this kind of attention."

"What does he want?"

Tycho turned away to watch Abe Fletcher give a play-by-play of Mikey's attack.

I pushed my way out of the crowd and logged out of the VIP Lounge, but not before I heard Palmer say, "I have a feeling Kid knows something we don't know. She definitely seems to have the inside on the Unidentified. Anybody hear any rumors? We're listening."

I wanted to go find Ari, but I didn't want to miss my meeting with Winterson. I couldn't believe that it had only been a week since the Unidentified dummy splatted into the Pit.

Winterson looked relieved to see me. She got up and closed her office door, and asked me to sit in another chair, closer to the wall. I couldn't figure out why, until I noticed that her computer screen was blocking the surveillance camera's line of sight.

"How are you?" she said.

"Yeah, I know my scores look bad. I've been so distracted with other things that I—"

"There's nothing wrong with your scores," she cut me off. "They're higher than they've ever been."

I pulled out my notebook® and checked my page. What little schoolwork I'd done since getting branded had been worth twice as much score. And the time I spent in the VIP lounge had to count for ten times as much skill compared to other workshop log-ins. "That has to be a glitch," I said, trying to figure out how much score credit I would get at this rate by the time I finished playing the Game.

"They reward what they value," Winterson said simply.

"But that can't be right. Is this fair?"

"Fair to whom?"

"If it's not fair to everyone, then it's not fair at all, is it?"

Winterson laughed. "I know it's crooked, but it's the only game in town."

"What?"

"Sorry," she said, seeing the look on my face. "It's a quote from a famous gambler and con artist. I didn't mean it. I wouldn't be here if I was really that cynical."

I closed my notebook®. "Do you know what happened to Mikey? Why he isn't . . ." I swallowed. "He didn't get Game Over, did he?"

Winterson checked her screen. "The administrators put his game on pause while Protecht continues with its investigations. As long as they don't find anything incriminating in his activity records, he should be back in the Game in no time."

I wished I felt relieved. But what if they found something incriminating? He was underage. With all the anti-laws any little thing could be evidence against anyone.

"Are your sponsors treating you okay?"

"Yeah, why wouldn't they be?"

"I just wanted to remind you that you can come to me if you need someone to talk to. Their best interests aren't always—"

There was an insistent knock on the door and it opened before Winterson could answer.

"Kid! There you are!" Anica said behind her pixie-grin. She turned to Ms. Winterson. "It's *so* sweet of you to show an interest in our player, Carol. Especially since you're already so behind on your own player schedule."

I squirmed, watching the two women stand off.

"Just making sure Katey knows I appreciate the opportunity I've had to get to know her. She's a good person and a hard worker." She looked at me. "A perceptive girl."

Anica interrupted her. "Thanks, Carol. But we're taking good care of her. She won't be needing your public access advising anymore." She gestured to me. "Come on, sweetie. There's someone I want you to meet."

I put my notebook® back in my bag and picked up my things. "Thanks, Ms. Winterson," I mumbled, and left with Anica.

29 INTERESTED THIRD PARTIES

"Would you like something to drink, dear?" Anica asked me when we got to her office.

I perched on the edge of an uncomfortable leather arm-chair. "No, I'm OK."

"But if you did want something to drink, what would you choose? Out of scientific curiosity," she said making a vague gesture in the air.

"Um, water?"

She looked deeply disappointed.

"Sorry," I muttered.

"Oh, you don't need to be sorry at all. You can't help but like what you like and want what you want, can you?"

She was being hyperfriendly again and it was freaking me out.

"I guess not?"

There was a rapid knock on the door behind me.

"There he is!" Anica said, getting up.

I turned and saw Anica welcoming Murdoch West into her office with two air kisses. I slumped down in my seat. "You know my friend Murdoch, don't you? From the Hit List?"

"We met at After Hours, actually," Murdoch said, the corners of his eyes crinkling with his smile.

"Anyway, we were just talking about you this morning." Anica laughed. Her smile was so wide it made my cheeks hurt.

"Well, actually, *everyone's* been talking about you," Murdoch clarified. "According to our research, the topic of seventy-eight percent of all conversations taking place since the Game opened today have been about you, Kid."

I was shocked, but I didn't know what shocked me most, that they had the ability to do real-time statistical research on random conversations or that so many of the random conversations were about me.

"I take it you didn't know you were so popular." Anica winked.

"Oh, I don't think popularity really has much to do with this," I mumbled.

"It doesn't matter, Kid. You've got buzz. I don't think you appreciate how special this is," Murdoch said, smiling.

"I guess not," I said quietly. I could've used a drink now, my mouth was feeling dry, but I was too weirded out to ask for anything.

"So we were reviewing your content, and Kid! I didn't know you were a producer as well as a spotter!" Anica said, practically pinching my cheek. "You're just so full of secret surprises."

"Your tracks," Murdoch began. "Your tracks are really . . ." He made an enthusiastic gesture when words failed him.

"What tracks?" I asked, rubbing my cheek.

"I really liked 'Last Laugh,'" Anica spoke up. "I could totally imagine it being played over a fun-loving photomontage for a Trendsetters ad spot."

"But those, aren't . . . those tracks aren't . . . available. I never put them up on the Listening Library."

"All work produced in the Game is available to sponsors for promotional purposes," Anica said.

"No offense," I said to the Hit List rep, "but I never signed a contract with you."

"Oh, I know," Anica answered. "But we have the right to share your information with trusted third-party companies. It's in the contract."

Murdoch leaned in. "I don't understand why you wanted to keep your talent hidden from us. We want to use your work in national campaigns, Kid. You'll get great exposure. Who doesn't want that?"

"I need to discuss this with my bandmates, you know? It's not totally up to me."

"Oh, yes. We completely respect the practice of consulting with friends before making important purchasing decisions," Anica said, smiling at Murdoch.

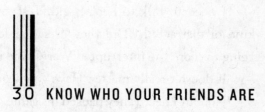

30 KNOW WHO YOUR FRIENDS ARE

I logged out of the VIP Lounge and found Tesla lurking by the entrance.

"Hey," she said, holding out a bag. "I'm sorry about the mix-up at After Hours. I didn't know . . ." She trailed off. "Here's the things you left at Ari's."

"Oh, thanks," I said. "Where is she?"

I scrolled through sponsor messages looking to see if Ari had responded to the texts I'd been sending her all weekend.

#spons: gas density experiments with He, SF6, N20 in Making Sense.

#spons: hungry? the Vending Machine's got what you want.

#spons: blink-of-an-eye technology testing stations installed in the Arcade. focus your brain for score.

But nothing from Ari. I hoped she was okay. How could she go the whole morning without updating her stream?

"I need to talk to her," I said. Tesla was acting weird, kind of distracted. "Did they ever decide on how they're going to score the interrupted War Game match?"

"It doesn't really matter. Have you heard from Mikey?"

"No, but I heard they paused his game. I was going to see if Ari wanted to drive by to see him after closing."

"You know, I could give you a ride if Ari . . . can't," she said.

"Good game," I said.

Tesla looked like she wanted to say something else, but just said, "Yeah, text me." She headed for the escalators, then called out, "And I really am sorry."

"Don't worry about it." I wasn't going to stay upset about a misunderstanding at After Hours.

I went to stand in line at Culture Shock to get a burger. I didn't really want a burger, but I couldn't concentrate enough to order anything else.

"French fries, *see voo play*?" I said hopefully.

"*Pommes frites*," the lady said, chuckling. "But they aren't French, so here you go, honey."

I took my tray and looked around for a place to sit. And there was Ari.

She was sitting with a flock of Craftsters on the far side

of Culture Shock, wearing a black UnID logo tee, sipping miso and looking at her intouch®. I weaved my way around the tables, trying not to spill my Poke® cola.

"Hey!" I said, sitting down a few seats away from Ari. "I thought you were dead. Or lost your intouch® or something. Did you hear what happened to Mikey?"

Ari didn't answer. She poked her sushi with sticks, and turned away from me to say something to Rocket. I saw that she had drawn the •–• across her wrist.

They were deep in conversation, I nibbled a fry. I looked around at the other Craftsters. They kept chirping like I wasn't there, which was kinda normal. They didn't ever pay much attention to me. But something was weird. There was something forced about their inattention. Even though no one was looking at me, they were more *aware* of me than ever before.

I stared at Ari, hoping that if I looked at her hard enough, she would look at me. *Look at me.*

"Look at me!" I burst out. Some kids from the other table glanced my direction and snorted. But the Craftsters stared at their plates, at spaces over my head. And Ari. She dipped a sushi roll in soy sauce and popped it in her mouth, her violet eyes never once meeting mine.

It wasn't hard to decode this behavior. I had been dropped.

So Ari wanted to play one of those girlie-games. Start a relationship war. What did I do for her to just put me on her "no empathy" list?

"This is effed up, Ari," I said, getting up and walking away.

I made my way up to the Studio on the fourth floor. I needed to listen to something, to drown out the intense silence I felt from people who I'd thought were my friends. Ari and the other Craftsters had blocked me from their streams, that's why my intouch® had been so dead.

Being in the Studio didn't make me feel better, though. I tried working on the "Last Laugh" track, but I couldn't stop thinking of Anica and Murdoch listening in, thinking up ways to use the music.

I got to the sample I recorded of Mikey laughing. It was his fake laugh at first, the one he did when he was fooling around. But I let the track play and listened to our conversation and heard my laugh. My real laugh. It felt so far away from how I felt right now. Why wouldn't Ari talk to me?

I turned it off and loaded another song. The track where Mikey played the bird-wing drum beat. I worked out a simple melody on the keyboard. I leaned close to the mic and whispered:

> I blow dandelion puffs into your yard
> Every day on my way home
> So that you'll remember me.

The Studio was the loneliest place in the Game without Mikey. I saved changes to *A Little Bird Told Me*, and got my stuff together to log out before I started to cry again.

My intouch® buzzed. I hated myself for hoping it was Ari, but I did.

It wasn't her.

#pro_harrison: my office, ms. dade. @KID

"Hey," Jeremy called out to me. "Harrison's looking for you. Did you think we wouldn't find out?"

"I didn't . . . I just got his message." I was holding on to my intouch®. "What's going on?"

"I'd guess Protecht wants to know about your new friend." He held up his intouch® screen to me. There was a low-res image on the display, but the picture was plain to see.

It was me standing uncomfortably close to my Unidentified e-pal at the park last Saturday.

31 PASSWORD PROTECTED

"Where did you get that?" I whispered to Swift as we navigated the back hall of headquarters. "Have you been following me?"

"Not me," he said, taking my arm, not like a friend or a date, but like he was escorting me somewhere for questioning. "It was sent to me by someone who was 'concerned' that you were cheat-coding on me."

But no one knew I had gone to the city that day. Elle's Alibi had hidden my coordinates, and the coordinates were in my private messages. No one could've seen them without my password. . . .

"Yeah, your friend Aria sure is considerate."

Would Ari do something like that? Use my password to

read my messages and then go to the coordinates to see who I was meeting?

She would, and did. Then sent the picture to Jeremy.

Harrison was stone-faced when we entered his office.

"What did I tell you about your passwords, Ms. Dade?" Harrison said quietly. "Do you know what it looks like to have the Network page of one of our very own agents compromised?" The vein in his neck reminded me of the stress meter in Jeremy's Buy, Sell & Destroy game. It was throbbing purple.

"In light of the recent incident at the War Game, a Ms. Knowland felt it her duty to keep us updated on suspicious behavior she noticed on your Network page. She's a friend of yours, I take it?"

My eyes started to sting, hurt and embarrassed tears, like red ants itching their way down my cheeks. I had trusted Ari with everything, including my password. I wanted to change my account settings immediately, to hide, to not feel this stupid and vulnerable.

"Who is he?" Harrison pointed to the picture.

"I don't know."

"This is the anonymous person you've been corresponding with, and you agreed to meet. What's his name?"

"He never told me." And for once I maybe understood why he hadn't. He didn't really trust me to keep his secrets.

Harrison made a deeply frustrated noise, and loaded Profile. He entered all the physical attributes he could make out from the poor quality photo. Light brown hair.

Dark brown eyes. Athletic build. Final level. Mixed race/ethnically ambiguous. Harrison kept tweaking with other settings, but there were still hundreds of matches and none of them him.

"He's not there," I said, more curious than anything.

Jeremy asked if he could try, and took control. Protecht didn't brand him for nothing—apparently getting a young Crackhead to work for you wasn't without its benefits. Jeremy redefined the search parameters, systematically narrowed and widened alternatives to pull up new results.

When he changed AGE: FINAL LEVEL to AGE: GAME COMPLETE, a familiar face flashed on-screen. I held my breath involuntarily, but Harrison picked up on it.

"Go back," he barked. And Jeremy pulled up the details.

The picture didn't really look much like him. He looked fresh-faced and innocent. Instead of the dread mullet, his hair was close-cropped. It was only the grin that gave him away. He should trademark that dimple.

"That's him, isn't it?" Jeremy said, pointing to one of the surveillance screens that was playing back the footage of the War Game fight. "He's the one who ruined the War Game."

I didn't answer. I just watched the replay of the fight. It looked like a horribly choreographed dance without the sound. So unreal at this distance.

"Brenton Kant. Completed the Game two years ago with high scores. He's nineteen." Harrison read off the stats. "Lives in Center City. Employed by Zeronet."

"I didn't know," I mumbled.

"Why are you protecting him?" Swift said angrily. "After what he did to Mikey?"

Harrison put a hand on Jeremy's shoulder, then spoke softly to me. "You know, your friend Mikey could get into a lot of trouble for all of this. I'm afraid Mr. Littleton has a record, a rather serious record, and more than enough suspicious activity to build a case against him if someone has information they're not sharing with us." He turned me toward the screen again. "This Brenton Kant character is dangerous. Anyone who bypasses the age-restriction security sounds like a predator to me. Are you afraid of him, honey?"

"I don't know," I said again, trying to figure out why all this was happening or what to believe. "But I know Mikey wasn't involved in any of that."

"I'm sorry, Ms. Dade. If that's all you *know*, there's not much we can do to help your friend."

I looked at Brenton Kant's Profile again. Why did he drag Mikey into whatever he had planned?

It wasn't that I couldn't be trusted, or that I was loyal to my brand. I just . . . I had no reason to protect someone who would hurt Mikey.

"He's planning something," I said, staring at Brenton Kant's clean-cut Profile pic on the screen. "He called it a pariah virus."

Harrison and Jeremy launched into action.

"We need to scan the system immediately," Harrison said. "Alert the administrators that we're going to need to renegotiate terms with Network Inc. We'll need increased resources to combat this threat. . . ."

32 FOLLOW ME

I went to find Tesla in the DIY Deopt.

"Is your offer still valid?" I asked her. "Can I get a ride?"

"Yeah, of course," she said, clearing away her project.

"Are all those heartthrobs?" She had a box full of electronics by her workspace.

"Um, yes. I get a little obsessed with mind-numbing tasks when I'm stressed. All that labor-intensive busywork keeps me sane."

We were heading toward the exit when she asked, "So . . . you talked to Ari?"

"I talked to her. She didn't really say much back to me."

"Strange. She had a lot to say *about* you on Friday night," Tesla said sarcastically.

We logged out of the Game and I imagined Ari and Rocket and the other Craftsters last Friday night playing their Truth-or-Dares. Leaving nasty comments on that *Rate It!* entry. Logging into my Network page and reading my conversation with Mikey. Seeing the coordinates mail from Brenton Kant and waiting for me there, spying.

Laughing the whole time. The "Last Laugh."

Once we were safe inside Tesla's car, I said, "She sure had a lot to say to Protecht, too."

"What?"

I told Tesla about how she gave my password to Protecht.

"Have you ever heard of a pariah virus?"

"I don't think so. What's its damage?"

"It sends out all the stuff you say about people behind their backs to the people on your contact list. Stuff that's supposed to be private. It's basically an automated Ari, I guess."

Tesla frowned. "I've never heard of any malware that could do that. That kind of destruction would require precision coding. I doubt even Jeremy Swift could code that. Where did you hear about it?"

"Rumors," I answered evasively. I wasn't proud of leaking the news to Protecht, and still felt like I owed it to the Unidentified to protect my sources.

"Um, I don't mean to alarm you," Tesla said, looking at her rearview mirrors again. "But I'm pretty sure we're being followed."

I looked back and saw someone turning onto the

residential road behind us. "Seriously?"

"I noticed it parked outside the Game. And there it is."

We were getting close to Mikey's already.

"Keep driving," I said.

"Oh, really? I usually pull over and drape myself seductively over the hood of my car when I'm getting tailed by creepy strangers," she said a little hysterically.

I twisted in my seat to get a better look. A familiar car was behind us. A car that had been idling in my driveway after my friends had ditched me at After Hours. "I know who it is," I said.

She relaxed her grip on the steering wheel a bit. "A friend of yours?"

"Not exactly. I kind of just revealed her boyfriend's identity to Protecht. So probably not."

We pulled into Mikey's driveway, and Cayenne's car rolled to a stop across the street.

Cayenne got out, and looked down the street.

"Why are you following me?" I called out.

"Come on. You should be used to it by now."

Yeah, I'd been followed before. By Protecht, by my mom, by Ari. All the kids at school watching my stream. All the sponsors never leaving me alone. It didn't mean I was used to it. "What do you want?"

"What's going on?" Tesla asked.

Cayenne looked at her, then said to me. "I need to talk to you. *Privately*."

I couldn't imagine what Cayenne Lewis had to say to

me. Especially since the last time I'd seen her in the prison warden's office, she barely even glanced my way.

"Why? I thought you said you were going to pretend I didn't exist?" I shot back.

"I heard your friends are already doing that," she answered. "It's almost trendy now, so . . . hi."

"Trendy. Right." I slammed the car door. "Not like *your* friends." I turned toward Mikey's house. "Sorry, I didn't buy the T-shirt, but I can't support an organization that smashes my best friend's face."

"Wait," she said.

I stopped.

"I don't know who else to talk to," Cayenne said.

I turned to Tesla. "Can you go tell Mikey I'll be right in?"

Tesla looked at the two of us, shrugged, and went up the path to Mikey's front door.

"What is it?"

"We didn't know," Cayenne said, watching Tesla disappear into the front of Mikey's house. "He didn't say anything about starting a fight, won't say why he did it."

"You mean Brenton Kant?" It felt good to see her flinch a little when I said his name.

"No offense, but I don't get why Kant is so interested in you," she said.

"He's . . . what?"

"I've asked him why, but he doesn't say. He's keeping secrets from us."

I looked at her. She was so pretty up close.

"Aren't you two, like, linked? Isn't he your boyfriend?"

Her eyebrows flew together. "That's not what this is about."

"Well, what is it about?"

"I was hoping you could tell me!" she shouted. "Forget it."

She turned away, opened her car door, and got in. But she hesitated instead of slamming the door behind her.

"I've gotten into situations by trusting people before," she said, staring at the asphalt. "I'm sure you know what I'm talking about."

I felt a knife-stab thinking of Ari.

She looked at me. "I don't like being suspicious of my friends, but I hate that I don't understand what his plans are. If you knew something, I hoped you would tell me."

"Why should I trust you?"

"You shouldn't."

33 CRIMINAL ACTIVITIES

"I should get punched in the face more often," Mikey said, his voice muffled through my hug. "Split and swollen lips make me irresistible to women."

"Shut up," I mumbled into his neck, but let go when I realized his ribs were still sore, and remembered we weren't alone.

Tesla was leaning against Mikey's parts-cluttered desk, instinctively sorting screws and tools into piles. Mikey's room resembled the JunkYard in so many unfortunate ways.

"What did she want?" she asked me.

"Answers," I said, clearing a spot beside Mikey on his bed. "She told me that Kant guy isn't telling anyone why he jumped you at the War Game."

"Could it be because he's vred?" Mikey said, picking up his controller and pounding the button like it had insulted his grandmother.

"She seemed to think there was something more to it than that," I mumbled, watching Mikey blast zombie mobs on-screen. "Did they say how long they're going to keep your game on pause?"

Mikey shrugged. "Probably until they find enough evidence to give me Game Over."

"Don't say that."

"We're underage," he argued. "They're just going to take whatever details they find as proof of our moral degeneration."

"No kidding. When walking down the street is breaking the law, surprise, surprise, we're all criminals," Tesla added. Then she frowned. "What are we listening to?"

Mikey was playing an old copy of the bird-wings track on the sound system. He didn't have the updated version I'd cut in the Studio today.

"A skeleton of a song," Mikey said. "The backbone beat."

"No. I mean, you had to give your notebook® back. You can't be streaming this from Network, right?"

Mikey concentrated harder on the game he was playing, pretending he didn't hear the question. It was what he did when he was guilty of something.

"Mikey, what did you do?"

He glanced at me sideways. "It was just an experiment."

"What?"

"At the Illegal Arts Workshop, after you left, they mentioned blind spots—these gaps where networks connect like digital synapses. Structures the systems don't notice because the information just makes the leap, but you could theoretically stuff data there . . . kind of concealed in the blind spot."

I wasn't following what he was saying, but Tesla looked intensely interested. "And?" she urged.

"And I played around with putting the theory into practice. I cached our songs in the cracks. They're hidden if you're not looking for them, but open access for anyone who knows where to find them."

"Show me," Tesla said, handing Mikey her notebook®. But I was upset. This was just the kind of excuse Protecht and the administrators were looking for to give Mikey Game Over.

34 EPIDEMIC

Protecht had issued a warning about the pariah virus on all channels of communication. All the screens were advising against even doing research on Archive. And the influx of intouch® announcements were particularly annoying:

> **#spons:** unauthorized programs more dangerous than ever. don't get infected, stay Protechted.

The hysteria quickly rose to critical levels with the It Listers fanning the flames of the rumor riots.

"I heard everyone is already infected, just that Protecht hasn't been able to detect it," Palmer Phillips was telling Abe.

"Maybe *you* are," Abe shot back. "It's like a social disease and you're a man slut." Palmer punched him in the arm. It was how Team Players punctuate their sentences.

"I can't even imagine what would happen if all my correspondences with Élan became public," Echo Petersson complained as her brand representative winked at her from across the VIP Lounge. She lowered her voice and whispered to Eva, "And think of what would happen if that thing you said about Quelly that one time got back to her?"

Eva glared at her. "I thought you said you deleted that?"

It sounded trivial and ridiculous, just like anything Fashion Fascists said, but having recently had all my private content revealed by a friend, I knew how much stuff like this could sting.

Tycho was sitting alone watching the frenzy feed itself. I wondered how it felt to know that you were the cause of so much anxiety.

My intouch® hummed for my attention. I checked it even though I had been only getting sponsor messages now that Ari was ignoring me and Mikey was still on pause.

toy321: found something . . . suspicious @KID

I put my intouch® away and noticed Tycho watching me. *Thank you*, he mouthed from across the room.

I logged out of the VIP Lounge, not really understanding what favors I'd done for Tycho lately, and went to find Tesla.

She was in the Arcade whispering with Elle.

"Hey, what's going on?" I said, approaching the Tech Help desk. I noticed Elle had tears in her eyes. She took her glasses off to dry them quickly.

"They're blaming Alibi," Tesla said quietly. "For transmitting the pariah virus. Everything is getting real serious real fast."

"I guess I shouldn't be surprised that they're using this scare as an excuse to crack down on unauthorized programs. I mean, they never go easy on these deliberate flaunting of Game guidelines. But I don't want to lose score for something I didn't do." Poor Elle.

"They haven't tracked Alibi back to you, though?" I asked.

"Not yet. But Protecht got more resources to hunt down its threats. Virus prevention is big business. They're out for results."

Tesla put her arm around Elle to comfort her. "This is so vred," she said. "I hadn't even *heard* of a pariah virus before you mentioned it, Kid."

That's what everyone had been saying. They'd never heard of it, and then all of a sudden there were warnings everywhere.

I opened my notebook® and did a quick search on Archive for pariah virus.

There were tons of results, but all of them really recent reactions to the crisis. The first mention was also the top hit for pariah virus prevention. Zeronet:

The pariah virus exploits a natural vulnerability in the Network system. Contact list transparency and mainstream connectivity practically invite the breach of confidentiality the pariah virus threatens.

Largely undetected from market malware scanners, there are no diagnostic systems available to determine whether or not a Network account is infected. The virus quietly catalogs all password-protected files and keyword searches, then sends sensitive content out to the least appropriate recipient on the account's contact list.

No one has yet determined what triggers the attack phase.

Currently, the only known prevention is to delete all contacts for an undetermined amount of time until the virus runs its course.

Of course, very few of us can afford to remain offline for any length of time. For uninterrupted service, switch to Zeronet, the alternative connection with increased privacy control.

Zeronet. Everyone has something to hide.

I shut my notebook®, disgusted.

I noticed Swift playing at a port in the corner. He was using the new blink-of-an-eye technology that was being advertised everywhere. The setup kind of looked like Tesla's flipstream goggles, but instead of magnifying upside-down-looking eyeballs, his eyes were hidden within a thin, green mesh grid over dark shades.

I walked over to the port where Swift was playing Buy, Sell & Destroy.

Swift was bobbing and weaving his head around to avoid the fist punches of aggressive and stressed-out stockbrokers in the Wall Street trading pit.

The new tech incorporated eye-movement tracking and blink-click interface in the design. I couldn't see Swift's eyes behind the shades, but it was weird to see him leaning back in his chair, twitching in front of the screen, hands gripped uselessly on the edge of the desk.

He was scary-skillful with the new technology.

"Has Protecht been able to detect any sign of the pariah virus?" I asked him.

"Not yet. But we will. Network Inc. is dedicating full resources to combat the virus and repair the security breach."

I looked at his game. He was a billionaire, and instead of button-mashing to shred sensitive documents, he had to rapid tweaker blink to pass the level. His stress meter was flashing red panic.

"Why isn't Mikey back in the Game yet?" I asked. "You know he wasn't responsible for that War Game riot. I told you who was."

Swift didn't answer.

"Look at me."

"I can't. I need to pay attention to what I'm doing now. The federal government's getting involved. If I don't play this right, they're going to start regulating."

I got pissed off. "This isn't a game." I tore off his goggle controllers.

Swift's businessman avatar fell down on the screen. Heart attack, the pressure was too much. Swift exploded into expletives. Then he turned to stare at me, angry and bleary-eyed.

He stood up and shouted in my face, "You ruined my game! I lost a life!"

"You're vred," I said, taking a step back. He couldn't tell the difference between what was part of a video game and what was not. He moved close into my space, close enough to kiss me, but the closeness was more threatening than intimate.

"Protecht hasn't completed its investigations," he said in a low voice. "No one's secrets are safe."

I logged out and headed across the parking lot to the Game shuttle pickup spot. I saw Ari sitting on the hood of her car. I was surprised when she saw me too and jumped down, walked over to me.

"Do you hate me?" she asked in the way she always did when we had a fight.

Yes. My brain knew this was an easy question, but I still didn't know what to say. I missed her, but I hated that I missed her. I couldn't believe she could just walk up to me like nothing happened.

"Everyone's been talking about you," she said when I didn't answer.

Yeah, I wonder why that is, Ari.

I couldn't do this. I wasn't going to be able to have a conversation with her without losing it.

"Ari, what do you want?"

"Nothing. I just wanted to make sure that we were still friends."

I opened my mouth to speak, kind of choking on my shock. "How could you think we're still friends? *You* were the one who dropped me, remember? You told Protecht my password and you ditched me and I didn't do anything."

"Yeah right, you didn't do anything. You only took credit for my searches, and ignored Rocket in the VIP Lounge and didn't tell her about what was going on with Palmer and Eva, and kept me from being branded by Hit List, *and* stole Jeremy Swift when you *knew* I liked him."

I didn't know Ari liked Jeremy. I mean, she acted that way about all branded guys, so excuse me if I didn't take her infatuation seriously. She could have him. The overambitious backstabbers would make a lovely couple.

"Besides . . . you should be *thanking* me," she said. "Do you think anyone would know your name if it wasn't for me?"

She was probably right. If she hadn't given my password to Protecht, I wouldn't have had to tell them about the pariah virus. And people wouldn't be talking now.

I looked at Ari. Half her face hidden behind her bangs. Thinking that her cruel betrayal was just part of the Game.

35 ZERO FRIENDS

I wanted to talk to someone. To not feel this alone in my room with my dog. But it was a Friday night and Mikey's page was still suspended. And even if she wasn't flirting shamelessly with cool hunters at After Hours right now, there was no way I could ever confide in Ari. I held my intouch® but there was no one to listen.

I checked the Network rankings. There were hundreds of names listed on-screen, all followed by strings of the emptiest of non-numbers. Nationwide, kids were dropping out of Network because of the pariah virus scare.

This whole attack plan hadn't been a revolutionary action, a way to fight back. It had just been a cleverly disguised Zeronet campaign, a plan to cut into their competitors' marketshares. Zeronet was positioning themselves on top while everyone was racing to the bottom.

All these zeros had to add up to something.

I thought about how I'd used this same ranking page to find the members of the Unidentified only a few weeks ago. Even their identities were buried in the Zeronet privacy trend. If I would've done the same search today, I never would've found them. Elijah Carmichael, Sophia Carvalho, Cayenne Lewis. Just a part of nothing.

I wondered if they knew they were involved in a Zeronet business strategy. I sat up in bed.

Did the Unidentified know?

Cayenne had come looking for me at Mikey's because she was convinced Kant was keeping secrets from the Unidentified. She was probably the only one who could understand what I was feeling right now. This feeling of being used. Cheated.

I wished I could talk to her, but I didn't know how.

Even though I hadn't erased my contact list as part of the virus scare, Katey Dade had zero friends.

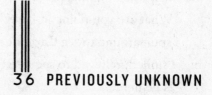

36 PREVIOUSLY UNKNOWN

I didn't know if I would find them there or not, but it was the only place I could look.

I used Alibi to synch my intouch® and headed out into the Saturday early morning calm to break into a prison.

It stood in the city center, a massive stone monument, but almost invisible. No one noticed it anymore. It was just in the background while everyone went around living their lives.

I found the grate Kant had opened; he had shown me the way. Or I thought he had. It was embarrassing to remember how I'd felt then compared with what I knew now.

The loose rocks in the tunnel whispered quietly with my footsteps. What if he was waiting on the other side?

Would he be as charming now that I knew his secret?

I stood crouched in the underground. Should I move forward or go back? I didn't want to go back.

Inside the prison yard, I retraced the steps I'd taken when I'd followed him. I was about to push open the door to the administration building when I heard a voice behind me.

"What are you doing in here?"

I spun around to see Cayenne standing in the gray morning. I smiled, relieved to see her. She didn't smile back.

"Is he here?"

"Why are you looking for him?"

"I'm not. I was looking for you."

She watched me, her face neutral. "Well, you found me." Then she turned back toward the watchtower. She stopped and looked back. "You coming?"

We climbed the creeping stairs. "What's up here?" I asked, panting a little.

"Nothing. Better reception," she mumbled. The room at the top was just as trashed as the rest of the prison. Small panes of glass were knocked out of the window overlooking the yard like missing teeth.

Cayenne walked to the window where she'd left her notebook® running. "What are you doing here?" she asked again.

I didn't know where to start. "Have you ever heard of Zeronet?"

"Please leave the promotional content out of this conversation, thanks."

"I'm not—" I hated that she always made me feel so under attack. "I think Brenton Kant is working for a company called Zeronet," I snapped. "This is entirely relevant."

She looked up from her notebook®, her full attention finally on me. There was something almost scary about the openness of her features, how vulnerable and delicate she looked. I almost wished she would go back to being a defensive bitch. "How do you know?" she asked softly.

I told her about how Zeronet was rising in rankings while everyone else was dropping out. How Protecht had a file on Brenton Kant that said he had completed the Game and was employed by Zeronet.

"I still don't know why he attacked Mikey," I said, thinking back to the security footage replay. "Why he had to be involved."

"To get you invested," she said numbly. "So you'd spread the word."

"What?"

"I couldn't figure out why he confided in you all the details about the virus that day." She nodded toward the administration building. "He kept saying he could trust you to do the right thing."

I was still confused and it must've shown.

"He knew you would tell your sponsors about it to protect your friend," she said. "You did, right? You told them?"

I didn't want to admit to her that I had sold them out, but the truth was obvious when I blurted, "But *why* would he want me to inform Protecht?"

She looked back at her notebook®, stared at her screen for a long time, then she stood up. "He had been hyping the virus the whole time. Saying how we should spam the Network with an invitation to a protest party with this sneak-code buried in it." She continued, spitting out her words. "But he kept on wanting me to rewrite the invitation, to tell people they had been infected by this thing and I didn't understand how he expected to get people to our event right after we oh-by-the-way effed up their Network status."

"I never got an invitation," I said.

"No. We never sent them out. This pariah virus thing took off on its own and—" she stopped and looked at me.

"It's a hoax," I said hollowly.

This was all my fault. All the hysteria about the pariah virus started when I'd mentioned it to Harrison.

I had been played.

37 SECRET'S OUT

"Do you guys have a Bat-signal or something?" I was in the passenger seat of Cayenne's car again, heading to Mikey's, where the Unidentified agreed to meet us.

"Who do you think we are?" Cayenne said, checking her mirror. "I just texted them."

We pulled into Mikey's driveway where Lexie and Tycho were waiting. "Why are we meeting here?" Lexie wanted to know.

"Mikey's mobility has been limited to his family's property since his game was put on pause," I answered.

"Yeah, but why does he—?"

"He's as involved in this Zeronet conspiracy as we are," Cayenne said before I could. "It's only fair."

Lexie shrugged.

"Have you heard from Elijah and Sophia?" Cayenne asked Tycho.

"Sophia's having problems getting out here, so Elijah's going to stop by and assist. He said he'd race here direct after."

I could tell Mikey was more than a little weirded out about having the Unidentified in his bedroom. But he hid it well.

"I haven't ever even *heard* of Zeronet," Tycho said, shaking his head.

"Oh, but I bet we would have," Lexie said. "When the time was right, hype at its highest, a big reveal of the anti-Network company. Promising privacy for whatever price."

"And we would've bought it," Cayenne said. "Because we are a target market." She paused, then asked me. "Do you think Trendsetters was in on it?"

"I don't know what to think anymore. But probably not. They thought it was genuine dissent they were tapping into. . . . I don't think they knew they were popularizing a Zeronet campaign."

Mikey's mom knocked on the door. "More of your friends here to see you," she said. Elijah and Sophia came in the room behind her. "Is everything OK?"

I smiled at her. "Yeah, we're fine," I answered. "Just missing Mikey."

Mikey looked at her and shrugged. Everything about Mikey's smile made him look guilty. She closed the door behind her, properly suspicious.

"I wonder what your mom thinks about a flash mob of friends showing up on your doorstep on a Saturday morning," I teased him.

"I don't know. But I doubt she would deny a prisoner his visitors. She's been arguing with the administrators to let me play again." He did a devastatingly perfect impression of her. *"It's not fair for my son to be under suspicion for being on the receiving end on some bully's knuckles."*

"We're all under suspicion for being on the receiving end," Sophia muttered.

"We're all under suspicion, period," Cayenne said with such finality that it was true. "I just . . ." Her eyes were wet and bright with frustrated tears. "I don't want to believe it's impossible to do anything real. *We* weren't a part of the Unidentified to be a fashion trend or a viral marketing sensation. We wanted to send a message."

The mood in the room was still less than convinced.

"Well, then let's send it," I said.

The Unidentified sent out an invitation.

We didn't use Network. Well, we did *use* it, but not in the way their corporate headquarters expected us to. Tesla and Elle had been freestyling with Mikey's code, the one he developed to cache our music in the unused online spaces, and expanded it to mark available hidey holes in the same way Tesla's empty parking lot locator worked.

We set up an UnID page that sponsors or Protecht or

Network administrators themselves couldn't even see, let alone monitor. Elle tried to explain it to me.

"You know what a mirror site is, right? Well, this is like a shattered mirror site, the shards of info hidden here and there and visible when a user follows a link. The pieces look like they're reconstructed, like you can see it and interact with it, but it's like an illusion. Multiple projections from separate locations that combine into something complete, but still a reflection of something untouchable."

I was just going to have to trust her.

People who dared to follow the link to the hidden UnID page in the face of the pariah hysteria were given an invitation.

You are invited to a party. You and everyone you know. It doesn't matter if your haircut is genuine or ironic. It doesn't matter if you haven't seen that film everyone's talking about. It doesn't matter if you would rather be left the hell alone. It doesn't matter if no one else is doing it. It doesn't matter if you don't have anything to wear. It doesn't matter if your friends think it's stupid. The pariah virus is just a hoax designed to keep us disconnected. You are invited to a party. We want you to come.

Where: The parking lot outside your local Game site.
When: Fri 20:00.

The secret's out.
Love,
the UnID

We spammed the entire Network with it, and the word-of-mouth whispers turned to shouts.

This was going to be epidemic.

38 THE ONLY GAME IN TOWN

We sat in the Arcade, watching responses pour in from around the nation. Thanks to the mainstream momentum from the ridiculous Unidentified craze, we were getting so many clicks. People were so interested in finding out what the Unidentified had planned that they ignored the hyper-precautions about the pariah virus.

"I'd like to take a moment to thank our sponsors," I mumbled, staring at the screen.

Some of the comments on the UnID Network page were promising:

High-volt idea. My whistle rock band has only played secret gigs in our drummer's basement. We're ready to make a bigger scene. *by jkatz.*

Others disheartening:

Will there be more UnID merchandise at the party? I
LUVVVV U GUYYZ. Also, who are you? *by lilmissbigsis.*

But mostly, kids were using the UnID page to plan and
organize and give one another tips on how to pull it off.

Cayenne was letting people know how to subvert the
inevitable arrival of authorities to crash the party.

There's always a chance the party may be crashed by
uninvited guests. These individuals have a history
of being stinky and causing drama, so accessorize
accordingly. *by the UnID.*

I got an official message on my intouch®.

#sysadmin: you're scheduled for mandatory conference in
headquarters. report to sponsors for escort. @KID

"Oh no, guys." I showed them my intouch®.

"Are you going to go?"

"You do know the definition of *mandatory,* right?" I
snapped. My guts were twisted with nerves. I didn't like the
idea of stepping into that office with Harrison and Anica rep-
resenting me. I wished it didn't have to be a one-player game.

I put my intouch® away and thought of something. Or someone.

I told Carol Winterson as much as I could about my situation, which was more than I had told anyone before. She seemed particularly disturbed about Brenton Kant's status.

"Where is he now?"

I shrugged. None of us had seen him since the pariah virus scare had taken off. He was probably living luxe in his house at Shady Lane Estates and getting bonuses for making his underground marketing movement go mainstream.

Winterson frowned. "Let's go have that talk with the administrators," she said, standing up.

She led me into headquarters and hit the buzzer at the administrators' office.

"Carol," Dr. Grant said, surprised to see her with me. "We were expecting Ms. Dade to arrive with her sponsors."

"She requested that I attend this meeting with her," Winterson said formally.

Mrs. Bond raised one of those perfectly plucked eyebrows of hers. "I don't see why that is necessary. This is a partnership matter. Her sponsors have requested termination of their sponsorship agreement. Fraudulent security claims cost the Game not only credit, but reputation as well."

"As I understand it," Winterson interrupted, "Katey did not knowingly supply fraudulent claims to her sponsors.

She merely relayed information she believed to be accurate when her friend had been *threatened* with expulsion for an act he did not commit. She was acting well within her obligations under Game policy, and I'll reserve my opinions about whether or not Protecht Securities was acting within theirs."

The administrators exchanged an irritated glance. "Carol, your opinions on Game policy have rarely been reserved," Mrs. Bond sneered. "I don't believe this is an a appropriate discussion to be having in front of—"

"She shouldn't be kept out of discussing policies that affect her," Winterson argued.

They looked at me, all three of them. I was painfully aware that I hadn't said a word in this exchange, and also that there wasn't anything I *could* say. The things that determined how the Game was played happened so far away from where I had any influence. Places I wasn't allowed to be.

"That will be all, Ms. Winterson," Dr. Grant said, not looking at her.

"I came here to make sure—"

"Your services are no longer required," he said, cutting her off. He was still looking at me, calm and unbothered as he was ending someone's career. "Would you please accompany these gentlemen out?"

Winterson stared at him. Two young Protecht guards showed up in the doorway. Mrs. Bond had signaled them already. Winterson turned to leave before they could touch her. She said to me, "It's not the only game in town."

I watched her leave. It *was* the only Game in town, actually. The other locations were outside the district, but she wasn't going to be able to work in any of those if she was banned from the system. Score didn't transfer if you got Game Over.

"She didn't violate Game policy," I said, finally speaking up. "You had no reason to let her go."

"You don't know what Game policy allows," Dr. Grant countered. "Operation procedures don't concern—"

"Does it allow a competing company to do business on Game premises?" I interrupted. "Brenton Kant needed administration approval to get access on site. That's a breach in your agreement with Network Inc. Aren't they supposed to have exclusive rights to operate on the Game system?"

The expression on Dr. Grant's face fell a little before he caught it again.

"Is that why Mikey's Game has been on pause so long?" I continued. "You don't want the authorities, media, or Network Inc. lawyers to find out that something you authorized led to an onsite riot and the *assault* of a student—"

"This isn't how you want to play it, Ms. Dade," Dr. Grant said menacingly. Mrs. Bond put a hand on his shoulder.

"Investigations into Michael Littleton's case are just finishing up," she said, unfazed by my accusations. "He'll resume playing by Monday."

"That's it? I'm just supposed to ignore your error and not—"

"You can play nice or not play at all," Mrs. Bond said.

286

"What do you mean?"

"What we mean"—Dr. Grant sat behind his desk—"is that you seem to be forgetting that the Game is a *privilege*," he said.

"You should be grateful for the opportunities you're afforded here," she added. "We're not your enemies."

"But if you don't start showing some team-player spirit around here . . ." Dr. Grant looked at me solemnly, like he was disappointed in me. Like he hated that I was making him say the words. "We'll have no choice but to give you Game Over."

Mrs. Bond looked at me from across the room, her arms folded across her chest. "Make good choices, Katey."

39 FLASH MOB

It was Friday night and my mom wouldn't let me leave the house.

"I told you. No," she said. "You're not going. You lost your sponsorship from *both* your sponsors—"

"Mom, trust me? That was a good thing," I said, scratching behind Lump's ears. Cayenne was already on her way here with Mikey.

I'd "lost" my sponsorship benefits only because I'd demanded to be released from my contract and have the rights to my content restored to me. The administrators wanted to blame the loss of credit and resources poured into the pariah virus scare on me, but I had potentially damaging information about their business practices that could trace the responsibility back to them. We were in an uneasy stalemate. But who knew if that would last after tonight.

"How could you sabotage your future like that, Kiddie?" She turned her back to me so I wouldn't see her cry, but I heard it in her voice. "Is this Game Over?"

"Not yet," I said. I didn't even really understand why the administrators hadn't ended my game already. Probably because they'd rather keep me playing. As long as I was in the Game, I'd have to play by their rules. But that's what they thought. I knew too much now to go back to how it was.

My poor mom. She was still captivated by the easy life the sponsors were selling.

"Now you're just going to end up like me," she said softly.

I walked over to where she was storming around in the kitchen. I put my arms around her; she felt shorter than me. "Mom. I love you. There are worse people I could end up being like. I'll be fine," I said into her hair.

I heard Cayenne's two timid honks from the driveway. Then what I assumed to be Mikey leaning on the horn.

"Let me go. Please?"

I left the house before she could answer.

They wanted team spirit. And I was going to give it to them.

On our way to not–After Hours in Cayenne's car, I had that nervous feeling. That *what if I threw a party and nobody came?* anxiety, times one thousand.

But when we turned into the parking lot we saw that people *had* come, times one thousand.

The parking lot was illuminated with film-set lighting, Hollywood premiere–style spotlights cutting particle beams through the air for After Hours. But no one was going inside. A lot of people were wearing masks: surgical masks with question marks drawn on them, classy masquerade masks concealing their eyes but accentuating their smiles. One guy was wearing just a disposable plate with a •—• strapped over his face.

"I guess he took the 'It doesn't matter if you don't have anything to wear' line in the invite literally," Mikey said, putting his hand over my eyes. "Yikes."

I laughed.

Tycho had remixed my "Last Laugh" track and was bumping it full volume through the amps.

Tesla was there with the other Save the Princess teammates passing out heartthrobs to the crowd. She had employed the entire DIY Depot department to get them done in time. We had included a message on each of the heartthrob straps. People curious and clever enough to decode it would find access to the UnID swarm cache. Elijah had already edited a new video clue hinting at the location of the next unlawful gathering.

Everyone had the lights strapped to their wrists, and judging by the frequency of flashing, they were excited to be there.

I eyeballed the growing force of police hovering at the

edges of our scene. So far they were just standing there like an audience of plastic soldiers, watching us. The laughing crowds of underage kids reflected in their mirrored visors. Lexie was wearing a powder pink gas mask and showing the authorities authentic-looking permits from conflicting sponsors that she'd copied from her brother's files. She left them to sort out the details and returned to the party.

I couldn't believe how many people showed up. Had to be three times as many as After Hours and I figured there were probably kids from other schools here. People outside the system who didn't have Game cards to get them in. I wondered if the Pit was empty now. If the sponsor reps were waiting at their booths with their free shit wondering where everyone was.

Cayenne ran over and gave me a huge hug. "Are you having fun?" she called over the music.

I looked over at Ari. Cayenne followed my gaze, then said, "Come on. You don't have time for that. Help me pass these out." She gave me a collection of heartthrobs and I entered the crowd to greet our guests.

In the jostle of people, I thought I saw a familiar face. Or not even a face. The parking lot lights reflected blankly off the smooth, flesh-colored mask, but was absorbed into the darkness of the eyeholes. He looked even more menacing than he had at the War Game riot. He stood on the fringes facing me. I could imagine his smirk hidden behind the expressionless plastic.

Then he turned around. Jeremy Swift had tapped him

on the shoulder and two members of the riot-check authorities were taking him into custody.

"Oh, did Swift find someone not on the guest list?" Mikey said as if he didn't have anything to do with it.

Tycho had just started playing the "Background Checks" track. It sounded incredible to hear the tiny unnoticed parts of our everyday get amplified into full recognition. Hear it pulsing loud in the cool night.

Everyone was dancing.

"They're going to cut the power," Mikey said, holding my arm.

He pointed to the riot police sent here to break up our "illegal" gathering as the administrators promised.

"Then let's dance while we can," I said to him, and we joined the crowd.

This part of the track worked the low-level hum of the electricity wires behind the Game into an intricate bassline. A loop of the World Languages garble and dishes crashing in Culture Shock arranged with the idiosyncratic keystrokes and mouse clicks in the Arcade kept a crazy rhythm behind one exquisite, never-repeating birdsong melody trilling high above all of that.

Just when the song was ending, when all the background rhythms were fading back to let the starling sing its aria in the spotlight, the lights cut out.

Silence. All around us, the logo lights of the Game blinked out and disappeared. The parking lot got so dark not even the asphalt sparkled. Even the buzz of electricity in the wires overhead, that most people didn't even hear before, made themselves conspicuous by their silence. The quiet was intense.

I stopped holding my breath.

"What happened?" Cayenne whispered, not wanting to destroy the magical silence.

Tiny lights flashed erratically around us. For a second I thought it was the light of stars. That somehow with all the lights out, we could see them twinkling on Earth. But it was the heartthrobs.

"We routed the power from the Game generators," Mikey told her, catching my eye. "They had to shut that off to shut this down." The light from his heartthrob lit his face, though not as bright as his smile did. "Oops."

The strobe-blinking of the tiny diodes made people's faces stop-motion in the darkness. The way darkness. I was still shocked at how quiet everyone was.

They were all huddled tight together, sitting down, looking up. The lights that had left the buildings around us were still echoed in the starry sky. We could see them now in the perfect silence. We had turned off the Game. Even if it was only temporary, for this one moment they didn't have the power. We did.

I was about to go track down the other Unidentified to whisper-discuss our next move. But Mikey stopped me, the lazy pulsing of his heartbeat lighting up his face. "Put yours on," he said, and slipped a heartthrob around my wrist. He looked down at it, waiting expectantly for it to come to life.

He was still holding my hand. "Watch, we can make them beat the same," he said.

I stood with Mikey and watched the lights flash. They weren't synched at all. I moved to pull it off again, but Mikey said, "Wait."

He moved closer so we stood together, forehead to forehead. Hiding the light from the people who were checking out the sky.

"Watch."

My heartbeat was always just a little after his, but I watched. And we were together. And he waited.

And then, blink . . . blink . . . blink . . .

The tiny lights matched up and were flashing together. I laughed and stared, amazed. Our hearts were beating at the same time, Mikey's and mine.

And together they started to beat faster.

Mikey tilted his head just a little and kissed me lightly. He kind of missed my lips, his just barely brushing the corner of my mouth. But the place his mouth touched mine tingled with heartbeat electricity.

I smiled, embarrassed, and pulled the thing off my wrist. I still felt the pounding inside, though. The shocks and jolts.

I looked around at the faces looking up, faintly lit by random heartbeats now and then. The authorities sprang into action. Raising their batons, they began to beat a predictable rhythm onto their plastic shields and moved in to break us up.

Everyone sat so calmly, so silently in the dark shadows, not taking their eyes off the sky.

"Look at that," Mikey said softly, squeezing my hand.

I looked up.

Shit, there were a lot of stars.

GAME OVER

We are the Unidentified. Or maybe we're not. Maybe you'll never know who we are.

In one night, unauthorized parking-lot parties took place outside 243 Game sites nationwide. The Unidentified didn't do that, the people who participated did that. Some of the gatherings were busted up by law enforcement citing the underage gathering prohibition, but others kept going until the sky lightened and the parking lot lamps blinked out.

It doesn't matter if everyone is watching. Or if no one is. We are going to keep making noise. With the hope of one day beating the Game.

ACKNOWLEDGMENTS

Thanks to Maya Rock for the push and Alessandra Balzer for the pull; they are the forces responsible for making all these ideas book shaped and I'm going to owe those ladies forever. High-fives to the Musers for their nonstop support during the never-ending writing process, especially Brianna Privett at Utopian.net, Suzanne Young, and Ryan Gebhart. Thank you, Jeff Katz, for recommending that I read the YA book that led me to want to write them—I know you were just doing your job, but this is all your fault. I need to thank the friends who offered to read the early versions of this, and my apologies to those who actually did. And to all the anonymous artist-vandals and my secret partners in crime, thank you for the endless inspiration and for refusing to play the Game.